# The Rose & the Ring

## Book One

# Lady Rosamund

*Joyce Williams*

## DEDICATION

To my husband Paul, our children Devorah and Matt, Rachel and Adam, Tim and Brittany, granddaughters Luccia Grace and Mica Noelle and grandsons Owen Paul and Simon John--you fill my life with joy!

Cover art: *Destiny* by John Waterhouse



ISBN-10: 1503234843
ISBN-13: 978-1503234840

RECOGNITION:

To Devorah Nelson, www.storydoctor.blogspot.com, for her help with character development, story structure and editing; and to Aimee Stewart, www.foxfires.com, for creating the cover art for *The Rose & The Ring* series using public domain paintings by John Waterhouse. I am indeed grateful!

## AUTHOR'S NOTE

Recorded in my family's history book, which my grandfather Alfred Irwin Brandt translated from German into English, is the account of a Swedish commander who marched his troops across the frozen Baltic Sea to come to the aid of a European feudal lord under threat of attack by his neighboring landowner. In the ensuing battle, led by the Swedish commander, the enemy was defeated and his fortress was burned (*Brandt* means "one who took a fortress and burned it.")

The Swedish commander, my ancestor, married the daughter of the feudal lord (an only child). The Brandt family remained in northern Europe until my 13-year-old grandfather along with his 16-year old brother embarked on the S. S. Kaiser Wilhelm der Grosse and sailed to America by themselves, emigrating through Ellis Island.

Stimulated to do some research, I discovered that the Baltic Sea did, in fact, freeze solid only once in recorded history; the winter of 1422-23. The November 1976 issue of *National Geographic* documents this unusual phenomenon and refers to this period in history as "The Little Ice Age."

As a child I heard many stories told by my grandfather about his homeland and past. One of those stories was the gripping account of a lady who disappeared at a wedding; her fate was not discovered until many years later. I set out to combine historical facts with this unforgettable tale.

The research into my family history provided the basis for *Lady Rosamund* and the springboard for this seven-generation historical fiction series, *The Rose & The Ring.*

*"Where one drop of blood drains a castle of life,*

*So one kiss can bring it to life again."*

*--Brothers Grimm, Sleeping Beauty*

# PREFACE

June 10, 1405. Feste Burg, Pomerania.

Perched above a rugged cliff, a formidable stone fortress undergirded a look-out tower that stared unblinkingly over the Baltic Sea. The Tarragon, a Hansa sea cog anchored off-shore, basked in the morning sunshine. Unwittingly, the man and child walking along the beach ventured too close to the cliff in their quest for sea shells.

"Look out!" Captain Erik Branden shouted, grabbing the girl by the arm and jerking her to safety as a large boulder tumbled from the cliff and splashed into the water below. They both gasped for breath as a soaking blast of cold sea water showered them.

When the young captain released the child and stood her on her feet, she pinched her lashes tightly shut and scrunched up her pointed little nose. Giving her curly dark head an aggressive shake and wiping her small hands over her bare arms, she started to laugh.

The captain scraped a shaking, calloused hand across his dripping sea-bronzed face and shuddered. If he had not been looking up, Lord Schmidden's only child would be severely injured or dead.

He eased out his breath and lifted his eyes in thanks that she was alive and well—and merely soaking wet.

His gaze returned to the girl in time to see her bubbling laugh chased away by a full-body shiver; the sea water was icy cold in contrast to the sunny day.

"Let's leave our shells here and collect them later." Erik waved his hand toward their small pile of plunder resting on the sandy beach near a skiff. "How about we row out to The Tarragon and get you warm and dry. Besides, I need to see how the crew is coming along with mending the last sail."

Her dampness forgotten, the girl bounded across the sand and reached the skiff first. "I'll help you," she enthused, obviously eager to prove she had paid attention to his instructions of another day.

When Erik had secured the skiff to The Tarragon and followed the child's nimble ascent up the rope ladder, he gave her a final boost over the side and held her upper arm in a firm grip to insure she landed on her feet. When he had joined her on the deck, he directed her to the galley below, where he retrieved a man-size wool jacket from a leather-strapped wooden trunk.

"This should keep you warm," he said, clumsily draping the voluminous garment around her narrow shoulders. As he stepped back to consider the fit, his grin shifted into a wry smirk.

Catching the twinkle in his Nordic blue eyes, the girl dismissed her awkward appearance with one carelessly quirked dark eyebrow. "Suits me just fine." She was having too much fun to complain.

As an only child, and a motherless one at that, Lady Rosamund Schmidden been shuffled off to the nursery whenever she made a fuss. But the unexpected arrival of The Tarragon with its genial young captain and his crew had filled her heretofore wearisome days with purpose, and the young captain's attention infused her with a sense of personal significance.

"You remind me of Karina, my youngest sister," Erik praised her, administering a big-brother pat on the top of her head before defining his compliment, "You're plucky and brave."

Beaming at his approval, Rosamund latched onto his arm and clambered up the coil of rope that offered the height she needed to see the top of the table. Her eyes burned from the acridness of salt brine mingled with the smudge produced by the tallow oil from the big lanterns providing light in the galley, but her chin tightened with determination and she unflinchingly held her post.

When the captain's concentration turned to the line-marked Portolan chart secured on the table-top by large seashells that served as weights on each corner, curiosity made Rosamund bold. "What are you looking for?"

Straightening up from leaning over the map, Erik ran his long fingers through his blonde hair and pushed it back from his forehead. With an affectionate smile, he explained, "Ever since the storm damaged the riggings and tore holes in our sails, sending us off course, I've been studying the shoreline to determine exactly where we are." He drew his brows together as he stared at the map again. "Most of the Baltic shoreline is made up of broad, sandy beaches, but since your father's fortress sits above a cliff, I'd say we're right about . . . here." He pointed to a spot on the continental coast.

Rosamund caught the tip of her tongue between her lips and stared intently at the map for a moment. Then she awkwardly thrust her arm through the over-sized jacket's front opening, propped her stomach against the table edge, and leaned forward. She stabbed her index finger at a point about two inches below Erik's designated location and announced, "Then this is where I live—when it's not summer."

The Schmidden property included two fortified residences. Burg Mosel, their ancestral home, served as the family's primary residence, but in the spring, when food supplies ran low and the lavatories were foul, Lord Schmidden and Rosamund moved to Feste Burg, a weathered stone and mortar fortress erupting atop a craggy cliff on the Baltic Sea coast. For Rosamund, summers at Feste Burg meant a simple lifestyle and the freedom to roam independently up and down the nearby seacoast, often with her horse Pfeiffer for companionship. The servants remained behind to clean the living quarters and restock the wild game—which they dried or smoked.

Feste Burg, built nearly two hundred years before Burg Mosel, featured formidable walls and a towering round keep. Although it was originally designed as a lookout to detect sea invaders, it hadn't been used for that purpose since Rosamund's grandfather, Lord Leopold, was a boy.

Burg Mosel stood near the Schmidden's southern property boundary and was as elegant as Feste Burg was primitive. During Lord Schmidden's boyhood, its spacious rooms had regularly hosted guests for tournaments, games, and hunts, and on special occasions a band of traveling minstrels or a harpist had provided entertainment and brought news.

Erik opened his mouth to comment on Rosamund's observation, but he was interrupted by a swarthy-cheeked crewman who poked his shaggy, bearded head into the galley. "Captain, Sir?"

"Yes, Kjell." Erik acknowledged the sailor's presence.

"She's ready to go, she is," he announced.

Immediately, Erik pushed the shells off the corners of the sheepskin map. As he grasped the long side and began rolling it up, his sky blue gaze shifted protectively to the girl. "I'd better take you back before your father gets worried. Now that the mainsail's been repaired, we can be on our way. I've got a hold full of cargo to deliver, and we're almost two weeks behind schedule."

At the captain's words, Rosamund's cheeks paled and her dark blue eyes brimmed with sadness. Abruptly, she pushed away from the table and impulsively leaped off the coiled rope, but her distress made her clumsy and she lost her balance when she landed on the well-worn planking.

"Whoa, there," Erik said, grabbing her under her arms and steadying her on her feet.

Too young to conceal her sorrow, she reproached, "I wish you didn't have to go away. Can't you take me with you?"

Her plaintive cry evoked a tender smile as Erik freed one hand and raised her face with his curled fingers. "Chin up, my lady. Who knows, perhaps we'll come back this way again one day."

After a hearty evening meal hosted by Lord Schmidden, the crew offered up a round of toasts that ended with Captain Branden offering his services should his host ever be in need of them. When good-byes had been said all around, the men headed back to The Tarragon to get a good night's sleep in anticipation of an early departure the next morning.

Young Rosamund went to bed without protest, but she barely slept, determined not to miss The Tarragon's leave-taking. Climbing out of bed before it was light, she dressed quickly, grabbed a coat, and made her way alone to the beach. She scrambled up onto a huge boulder and waited, staring at The Tarragon, trying to fix the image in her mind so she would never forget it.

With its steep stem, straight keel, platforms fore and aft, a sixty-feet-high mast with a battle station at the top, and a single yard sail measuring eleven hundred square feet, The Tarragon was a masterpiece in modern workmanship, a vessel worthy of pride. And the painted dragon's head salvaged from a Viking ship that decorated the prow gave it distinction.

Just as the sun edged over the horizon, young Rosamund watched the crew come to life; she could hear them shouting, singing, laughing as they set the sails and raised the anchor. Shielding her eyes with one hand, she waved at the receding ship, alternating her arms until The Tarragon was reduced to toy-size.

When she turned her gaze away at last, Rosamund's dejected gaze landed on the forgotten heap of sea shells. With renewed purpose, she slid off the boulder and darted to the pile and dropped to her knees. As she lifted each mountain-shaped shell, she shook out the sand and debris and then arranged them in a row by size. Selecting the largest shell that was about the width of her small palm, she clutched it to her chest, got to her feet, and headed up the trail from the beach with single-minded intensity.

When she reached the stone stairwell leading to the look-out tower, she began the climb. The staircase was narrow and steep, forcing her to stop several times to rest, and by the time she reached the top, she was panting. However, a thrill of satisfaction rushed through her heart as she settled the cream-colored conical shell with its narrow, concentric circles in crimson, yellow, and purple on the wide stone ledge circling the outer wall below the window that overlooked the sea. As if protecting precious memories, she pressed her small hands on the top of the shell and gazed out over the water, steadfastly watching the speck that was The Tarragon until it disappeared from sight.

With a final pat, she left the shell on the ledge in the tower and headed down the steps, whispering under her breath, “He’ll come back for me one day; I know he will.”

October, 1422. Burg Mosel.

## CHAPTER ONE

Seventeen-year-old Lady Rosamund Schmidden kept her head down, but she struggled to discipline her grin as she watched Hilde Stone, the scullery manager, fix her narrowed eyes on Kathe, her marriageable-age daughter. Friendly and relaxed by nature, Kathe leaned against the door jamb, laughing easily with Ivan, the enterprising village youth who collected mushrooms in season and delivered them to the castle kitchen in exchange for a flitch of bacon, a leg of venison, or some other generous addition to his family's simple diet.

"That girl! What is she thinking?" Hilde muttered, pushing a straggling strand of gray hair back from her face. In the next moment she cast a wary glance at Lady Rosamund, her master's daughter.

Although Rosamund pretended not to hear the

older woman's frustrated lament, she couldn't help an inner chuckle. Grabbing up a flat-ended wooden *spathe*, she busied her hands scraping crusted porridge off the breakfast crockery into a handled bucket. Her intense vigor was the only visible sign of her repressed laughter.

Kathe Stone was the scullery's chief attraction for Rosamund, and even though the two young women were as different as wool and straw, they were fast friends. Although she was two years younger than the scullery maid, Rosamund had enjoyed many aristocratic advantages that made her seem older than her underprivileged companion. However, to her credit, she'd insisted Kathe be taught to read and write and included her in lessons as often as her mother would allow.

Hilde knew her daughter's exposure to a lifestyle that could never be hers carried with it the risk that her girl would be dissatisfied with her station in life. Nevertheless, Hilde saw herself in her daughter, and her own longing for more from life than the drudgery found inside the four walls of the scullery, with its endless dirty pots, crocks, bowls and cooking utensils, made her allow Kathe's friendship with Lord Schmidden's motherless daughter. However, to ease her conscience, Hilde tasked Kathe with the scullery's least desirable duties, and knowing what it cost Kathe to be her friend, Rosamund frequently volunteered to help the maid with her chores so the two of them could have time to study and play.

Rosamund finished scouring the final porridge bowl and rinsed her hands in the nearby cast iron washbasin. As she dried them on a ragged scrap of cloth, her gaze returned to her friend in time to hear the end of her conversation.

"Good-bye, Ivan. I'll see you next week," Kathe bid the enamored youth farewell with a broad smile that lighted up her whole face.

The moment the door closed, Hilde pounced. "You! As good as promised to our master's clerk—a step up for the likes of you—and you would throw it all away by flirting with that *boy*. I've a mind to lock you in the dungeon and throw away the key . . ." She sputtered, agitation leaving her breathless.

It was common knowledge that Lord Schmidden's red-haired Gaelic clerk, Curtis O'Donnell, had taken a fancy to the jolly scullery maid with the long brown braids and merry disposition that made her everybody's friend.

"Ma-ma! I was only being friendly. Besides, Ivan knows I favor Curtis." She lowered her eyes demurely even as her cheeks flushed a rosy pink.

"Naught with your excuses! Off with you . . . out of my sight. And you too, my lady! Take my girl away—and talk some sense into her silly head!"

A few minutes later, in the room Kathe shared with her mother in the servants' quarters, Rosamund turned her back to her friend, announcing, "I'm ready."

To keep her elegant gowns fresh and beautiful, Rosamund always borrowed a *cotte*, a homespun overdress, from Kathe and masqueraded as a peasant girl when the two of them slipped outside the castle wall to pick wild strawberries—or larkspur or snowbells—or to picnic along the river bank or wade in the water.

Kathe grasped the laces and cinched them as tightly as possible through the parallel grommets that straddled Rosamund's spine so the garment would fit her more slender figure.

When the girls had passed through the castle's

back gate, Kathe skipped along beside Rosamund, happy to be released from her duties, whatever the reason for the freedom. As they headed down the hillside, Rosamund suggested, "Let's pick some flowers for your mother—to cheer her. She seems seriously worried about you and that Ivan fellow."

Kathe rolled her eyes and groaned. "Her fretting is for nothing. Curtis spoke to your father last week. He gave us permission to marry and promised to announce our betrothal on Mid-summer. Curtis thinks I should tell my mother now, but I want it to be *our* secret for a little while." Her brown eyes begged her friend for understanding.

Two hours slipped by while the girls picked flowers, discussed Kathe's wedding plans, and ventured farther than they'd ever been before.

Rounding a low hill, they both saw the graceful doe standing beneath a tree at the edge of the woods across a flower-dotted meadow. The doe's head was lowered to the young fawn resting in the grass at her feet.

The girls immediately slowed their steps.

In the next moment, Rosamund thought she heard a slight rustling sound off to her right. A bit spooked, she put out her hand to stop Kathe's next step forward. They saw the doe raise her head; she'd obviously heard the noise too.

While the girls held their breath, fearing a forest creature, two men Rosamund had never seen before, one with a gun raised and aimed at the doe, emerged stealthily from the trees a short distance above them on the hillside.

Instantly fearing for the doe's life and equally incensed that strangers were poaching on her father's estate, Rosamund leaped forward. "You're trespassing!" she shouted. "This is Lord Schmidden's land."

As the men swung around, the gun shot off into space; startled by her outburst, the man had accidentally jerked on the cord that ignited the gunpowder.

Rosamund felt a swelling of justification and relief as doe and fawn bolted to safety in the woods.

Making no effort to disguise their hostility, the two men approached, cursing loudly.

Rosamund could see at a glance that the man carrying the gun was the younger of the two, a man probably in his mid-thirties. He was fashionably dressed and unsettlingly well-built. And his face was, without a doubt, the most handsome she'd ever seen. As their eyes met, a shock ran through her like a streak of lightning.

When he broke the connection, his intense gaze raked over her face and body in a wordless reminder to her that despite her ill-fitting *cotte*, she was a shapely young woman.

Even as she felt a blush creep up to warm her face, Rosamund was suddenly aware that the older man had cocked his head and was studying her through cold, dark eyes. His shrewd expression told her he'd not been fooled by her disheveled hair and shabby garments.

Although he was slightly shorter than the handsome man, every inch of his body radiated a predatory power. His skin was stretched tight over his sharp features and his thin lips held a fierceness that seemed barely held in check. Instinct told her he was far more dangerous than anyone she'd ever encountered.

While she stared at him, his jaw hardened. "And why would *you* be defending Lord Schmidden's property?" His voice was as cold as his eyes.

At his challenge, Rosamund's chin came up and her blue eyes sparked with pride and indignation. "Because I'm his daughter."

The younger man cleared his throat and shifted from one foot to the other, recapturing her attention as he scrutinized her from beneath black brows and a head of curly black hair. She had the uncanny sense that he was evaluating her, weighing options unknown to her.

Then he raised his dark brows, offered her an indulgent smile, and said in a mildly patronizing tone, "Of course you're Lord Schmidden's daughter—and I'm the King of France!" He chuckled at his own joke before he continued, "But this is *my* land, and *you* are the ones who trespass."

Rosamund felt slightly faint; could it be true?

"So my advice to you, *my lady*, is go back where you came from. And if you know what's good for you, don't come this way again." Although his tone remained mild, she felt like she'd been caught in his gun sight.

Kathe had remained silent, horrified by Rosamund's brash boldness, but now she grabbed her friend's arm and tugged urgently. "Please, my lady, let's go." Desperation and fear laced her low words.

"Remember, you've been warned." The older man's gravelly caution felt like a threat and sent a chill through Rosamund that set her to trembling.

Kathe jerked her friend's arm a second time, but it took a moment for Rosamund to find her legs before she grabbed her companion's hand and they started to run.

Rosamund's mind raced. She knew they shouldn't have wandered so far. And she should have paid closer attention to the time. She looked down at the flowers still clutched in her free hand; with the life squeezed out of them, their limp heads drooped over her tense fingers in a wilted mass. The unexpected encounter with those two forbidding strangers had left her feeling as wilted as the sorry bouquet. She tossed the flowers aside and rubbed her sticky hand down her skirt, as if to wipe away the disturbing encounter.

When the girls finally reached the trail at the base of the outcropping leading up to Burg Mosel, they stopped to catch their breath. Holding their heaving sides and gasping for air, they stared up at the blue flag flying proudly from the pinnacle of the highest-reaching tower, proclaiming "All is well!" to everyone who looked to it for reassurance. It was a welcome sight indeed.

Finally Kathe gasped out, "What were you thinking, shouting at those men?"

Rosamund tightened her chin defensively. "I didn't want them to shoot the doe . . . and besides, poaching is a serious crime." Not for the world would she admit to Kathe that she'd been terrified—and thoroughly intrigued.

"Well, the next time you decide to play the heroine, leave me at home. I want to marry Curtis, not be dragged off to some dark lord's dungeon. Or worse, his bedroom."

When Rosamund stared straight ahead and didn't reply, Kathe flipped her long braid over her shoulder and cast a side-glance at her friend. "The handsome one certainly gave you the eye—and I'd say he liked what he saw."

Rosamund shrugged. No way was she going to comment; just thinking about the way that handsome man had looked at her made her feel weak in the knees. As the only heir to the Schmidden property and all the responsibility that entailed as protector for the many families living on their land, Rosamund knew she'd have to marry someone capable of managing her affairs, with or without love. But her heart couldn't help but dream of a handsome prince.

## CHAPTER TWO

Loud cries disturbed Rosamund's sleep. She sat up with a start, instantly curious as to what could be the cause of such a disturbing commotion. The voices and wails seemed to stem from pain or some other form of human suffering. Grabbing her robe from the end of the bed where she'd discarded it last night, Rosamund poked her arms in the sleeves and knotted the sash around her middle. Her toes slid into the house shoes she'd left on the wool rug beside her canopied bed.

Her nerves thrumming with anxiety, she dashed along the hall toward the broad marble staircase and pressed her face to the window that looked down on the stable yard. The sight that met her eyes sent a wave of nausea pushing up into her throat. At least two dozen peasants were clustered in the open yard. Some had bloody bandages wrapped around their arms, legs, or heads. Others held the ends of makeshift cots, carrying wounded women and children.

Rosamund, forgetting her state of dishabille, raced down the stairs and out the back door. As she rounded the end of the boxwood hedge, she nearly mowed down Curtis, who had heard the ruckus and was first on the scene.

"Go back to your room, my lady. I'll deal with this," was not the right approach to convince Rosamund to retreat, but Curtis didn't bother to make sure she followed his directive.

While her father's clerk hurried toward the disconcerting scene in the yard, Rosamund ran to the laundry, located at the opposite end of the kitchen from the scullery on the lower level, where servants were already busy taking advantage of the cool morning hours. Grabbing up a stack of neatly folded towels with one hand and a nearby bucket of hot water with the other, she dashed out the door.

By the time she returned to the stable yard, Curtis had managed to calm the distressed peasants enough to piece together their story. After Rosamund had helped him remove bloody bandages, wash open wounds, and apply fresh dressings, and the unexpected visitors had been sent to the servants' quarters for a meal, he related their woeful tale.

"Raiding parties have been making life miserable for the villagers along our border with Lord Frederick. Until today, we've only heard a few rumors, but these folks came for help, rightly convinced that Lord Schmidden does not know the severity of what's been happening."

"Of course he doesn't know; my father would never turn a blind eye to such abuse!" Rosamund's outrage made Curtis give her a cautionary glance.

She quickly lowered her voice, but her questions lost none of her intensity. "Who is behind these raids? And what do we need to do to stop them?"

"Lord Frederick and his estate manager—devils in the flesh—that's who. Lord Frederick is charming, and handsome enough to pass for an angel, and that Dagon is a demon if I've ever met one. One look from him is enough to put terror in the heart of the bravest of men!"

Shocked to recognize from his description the identity of the two men she and Kathe had recently encountered, Rosamund swallowed her consternation; obviously Kathe hadn't mentioned their frightening adventure to Curtis. And her own fairy-tale dream of having met prince charming suddenly took on the characteristics of a nightmare.

"Did anyone indicate Lord Frederick's motivation for these attacks?"

Curtis frowned. "They say Lord Frederick is in debt—maybe for that new fortress of his—and that he squeezes the life and livelihood out of his people, leaving them to starve. So they raid our villages, trying desperately to survive."

At her wide-eyed stare, he grimaced. "Sorry, I thought surely you had heard the gossip."

Rosamund chewed on her lip before replying. "The servants are pretty close-mouthed around me. And my father generally sees me as a child; I'm protected but left out when it comes to matters of governing. I guess that's what he has you for." Her words were a bit sharp, but her smile softened her comment.

* * *

"Check-mate!"

With an angry flick of his wrist, Lord Frederick

flipped the chess board and its hand-carved pieces into the air. “You cheated,” he accused flatly, glaring at Dagon as the chess pieces clattered to the floor.

“No, my lord.” Dagon’s thin lips grew thinner and his words held raw-edged honesty. “Your mind was not on the game.”

Lord Frederick hated being contradicted. “And why is that, pray tell?” He snarled, “I’ll tell you why. It’s because *you* have not managed to bring in enough money to keep the creditors off my back. I suggest you raise more taxes—or you will find yourself without your tongue.”

Dagon didn’t flinch at the gruesome threat but his voice and eyes were ruthless. “There’s no water in that desert, my lord. Your villagers are already pillaging across the border with Lord Schmidden—just to eat. You’ll have to tap another source.”

Lord Frederick’s head came up and his dark eyes kindled with interest. “And I suppose you have such a source in mind.”

Dagon shrugged. “I may have, my lord.”

“Well, out with it! Don’t keep me in suspense.” His mood swings would have aggravated a saint.

“Marry the girl.”

Lord Frederick shot out of his chair, demanding hotly, “Marry the girl! What girl?”

Without the flicker of an eyelash, Dagon replied, “The girl we met trespassing on your land.”

Staring at his estate manager as if he had suddenly grown two heads, Lord Frederick sneered, “And just how will marrying a peasant girl solve my financial difficulties?”

Dagon rolled his eyes and snorted derisively. “That aggressive girl wasn’t a peasant, you fool; she was Lord Schmidden’s daughter.”

“Lord Schmidden’s daugh . . .” Lord Frederick grabbed up the nearest chess piece and threw it at his manager. “Get out! Get out now! And don’t come back until you’ve got something more concrete for me than an empty joke,” he roared.

Dagon’s hand snaked out and he caught the flying king before it hit him in the forehead. His black eyes burned like coals in his dark face and his voice was low, gritty, and laced with sarcasm. “I’ll do even better. I’ll come back with a marriage bargain that will make you lord of the wealthiest estate in the land. And all you’ll have to do is be your charming self until the priest says ‘Amen.’”

October 1422. Burg Mosel

## CHAPTER THREE

It was a beautiful autumn afternoon. Not a single cloud disturbed the sky and the sun smiled an illusion of warmth over the far south-eastern mountain ridges. Lady Rosamund Schmidden gave Pfeffer his head and they galloped together as one, her long dark hair streaming behind her and the wind snatching at her breath. Plunging headlong into the crisp air, they left a ribbon of steamy vapor shimmering in their wake. Rosamund drank in the frosty air until her lungs ached and her worries were immobilized, chilled into silence.

The path she chose wound its way through the fertile valley and played follow-the leader with the river that wound along the south side of the outcropping. Colorful fallen leaves covered the landscape, and in symmetrical row after row, the quiet fields extended from the pathway. Dense woods covered the not-too-distant hills, and snow blanketed the majestic mountain peaks backed against the horizon. For a few brief moments the countryside blurred as reality faded to a muted shadow.

But the tower bell rang, interrupting Rosamund's brief reprieve just when it seemed they could go on forever. Gong! Gong! It announced the evening meal.

At the base of the outcropping she reluctantly slowed Pfeffer to a trot and turned him around. As they began the challenging climb back up to the imposing castle at the summit, reality settled down on her like a cloak and heaviness once again weighted her heart.

Pfeffer carried her between Burg Mosel's towering stone gates and they followed the cobbled drive along the front of the mansion. Sixteen grand stone steps led up to the front entrance, where jardinières overflowing with tansy and calendula defined the corners of the balustrades that flanked the massive double doors. Faced with worked iron that reinforced their strength, the oak doors were sturdy and intimidating. Etched into a broad, flat stone above the entrance, two guardian angels held court, their impassive faces never revealing that they kept a constant watch over all who arrived and departed.

Leaving Pfeffer to the care of a stable boy, Rosamund followed the stone path beside the shoulder-high box hedge and entered the mansion's arched back door. Rosy-cheeked and glowing from the fresh air, she hurried across the vaulted entry hall and down the east corridor. Moving past the dining hall where servants were busy setting up for the evening meal, she continued on to the great room.

When her father failed to look up to greet her, a frisson of fear tingled along her spine. She cast him a puzzled glance as she combed slim fingers through her tangled curls. The heat of the fire drew her, and she pulled a small stool close to the hearth. Bending low to sit on it, she smoothed the skirt of her brown riding *cotte* over her knees. Graceful as a willow bough, she leaned toward the blaze and stretched out her hands to its comforting warmth.

When her father heaved a burdened sigh, she turned her head to study him. His fists clenched around the lion's paws carved into the ends of the chair arms. Worry lines creased his face, and his dark eyes stared at the suit of knight's armor standing near the fireplace as intently as if it somehow held the antidote to his tension.

She caught a sharp breath. "Papa, what's worrying you?" The words slipped out before she considered the consequences of her question.

Startled, he lifted his leonine head. "What?" His blue eyes under bushy white brows abandoned the glinting armor to focus on his daughter. "Hmm? Oh, I . . ." he mumbled and shrugged. "It's nothing, nothing you need to worry about." He got to his feet and strode from the room.

Rosamund stared after him. She knew her father well, and despite his denial, she knew he was troubled—more troubled than she'd ever seen him. And even more worrisome, his anxiety seemed to be increasing from day to day. She shifted on the stool and shook her head. Poor, dear Papa. This was not the first time she'd made an attempt to share his problems. And just like each time before, he'd hastily escaped the conversation. What could possibly be causing him such distress?

Invincible, Papa had always been. Wise and gentle and doting. None of her girlish worries had confounded him. He could right each wrong and kiss away every fear. He adored her, and she delighted in pleasing him. But recently he'd been distracted and preoccupied.

The clatter of her father's heavy footsteps on the stone floor in the next room diverted Rosamund's puzzled thoughts. In one abrupt movement she stood to her feet, sending the small stool she'd been sitting on tipping to its side. But the clatter caused by its crash was not sufficient to distract her from her purpose; she clenched her hands into fists, drew in a sharp, bracing breath, and rushed out of the room.

As she hurried along the corridor she could see candlelight flickering through the glass panes in the header windows above the dining hall doors. Pausing in the slightly open doorway, Rosamund noted that one end of the long refectory table was set for two. The table's solid legs ended in clawed feet and vines were etched into the outer rim of its inlaid top that glimmered in the firelight. Gleaming mahogany paneling concealed the thick stone walls and provided an understated backdrop for several richly-hued tapestries. Shutters and dark blue silk draperies accented the recessed windows. Framed by elaborate moldings, the ceiling featured a central fresco of orange-throated blue swallows swooping among puffy clouds and baby-faced cherubs. The glow cast by the candles burning in the sixteen-arm chandelier suspended over the table colored everything a rosy amber.

Her father stood with arms locked over his chest as he stared blankly at the ornate-handled swords wielded by his great-grandfather when gaining possession of Schmidden territory that were mounted on the wall to the left of the fireplace. His shoulders were hunched, and his face, chiseled by shadows, betrayed his fear.

Mustering her courage, Rosamund stepped close enough to breathe in his familiar sage soap. Laying her hand on his arm, she reproached, “Papa, you’ve been anxious about something for days; I know you have.” When he frowned, she persisted, “I’m worried about you. Please, speak with me.”

His attempt to disguise his groan proved unsuccessful. “Oh, my dear, I didn’t mean for you to worry.”

She tugged lightly on his arm with both hands. “Worry about what, Papa?”

Turning toward her, he grimaced and sighed again. "If only your mama . . ." The loneliness in his tone made her heart ache, made her wait—hoping he would finish his sentence. But he didn't. He never did on those rare occasions when he mentioned her mother. Instead, he fixed his eyes on the pastoral scene depicted in the tapestry covering the wall behind her and changed the subject.

"Raiding parties have repeatedly attacked the villagers living along our border with Lord Frederick." His mouth twisted with frustration, "I've tried to make peace—without success, but now Lord Frederick has demanded . . ."

Rosamund's mental picture of the enigmatic Lord Frederick was rapidly followed by one of the injured villagers she had helped to bandage.

At her sharp gasp, her father shot her an oddly furtive glance, cleared his throat, and hastily rephrased his statement. "Lord Frederick is threatening to unite the neighboring lords against me." His voice faded to a harsh whisper, "If he succeeds, I'm not strong enough to defeat all of them at once." His drawn face and tormented eyes reflected his anxiety.

Shocked by her father's disclosure, Rosamund unconsciously held her breath as he continued.

"Winter will buy me some time, but by early spring I've got to have help." His big hands reached for her slender shoulders, his fingers tightening spasmodically as he confessed the underlying source of his distress. "This is my fault—all my fault," he groaned. "I turned my back on God when your mother disappeared . . ." His sentence trailed off as he stared at the fire.

Despite her dismay, Rosamund curbed her impulse to prompt him.

Finally, after a long silence, his voice seemed to come from a far distance. "I told God to leave me alone—and I forbade the servants to mention Him. I decided if He couldn't take care of my Rose, I couldn't trust Him with anyone else I loved? I was determined to care for you and all the families living on our land—without His help." He pressed his thumbs to his temples. "But I can't seem to resolve this situation with Lord Frederick." His words were sharp and clipped, with a bitter twist, "So . . . God has me cornered."

"Papa—" Rosamund began a loyal defense when

a servant bearing logs for the fire entered the room, interrupting their conversation.

"Don't give it another thought, my dear. I'm sure I'll find a solution." Lord Schmidden quickly downplayed the gravity of the situation, "I always do." He patted her shoulder reassuringly, then pivoted on his heel and strode from the room.

Overwhelmed by frustration and fear, Rosamund worried her lower lip and stared at the fireplace. But the flames, taunting her with their greedy hissing, offered no reassurance.

Servants brought the evening meal, but when her father did not return to join her, she ate alone, poking at her food with little appetite.

At last she gave up on her effort to eat and fled to her two-room suite on the second floor of the east wing, where she methodically prepared for bed. But she lay awake for a long time.

And when she finally fell into a fitful sleep, her dreams were disturbed by tormenting images of the handsome Lord Frederick chasing her down the marble staircase, his right hand brandishing a bouquet of wildflowers like a sword as he shouted, "Get out! Get out! Burg Mosel belongs to me!"

* * *

Burg Mosel lay deathly still, pinioned on its lofty perch. No moonlight shone down on its cobbles and turrets. No wind blew away the suffocating pall that wrapped it in a cloudy shroud. No light beamed out from the windows. The embers in the great room fireplace were dead. Rosamund's low stool still lay tipped on its side. And the decanters on the sideboard sat empty, drained to the dregs.

Lord Schmidden stared at the blank wall above the fireplace where a painting of his wife had once hung, and he sighed repeatedly—deep, painful breaths that sounded like they squeezed the life out of his heart. Frustration had long passed, leaving black despair in its place. The ghosts of his discarded ideas danced around him, their shrieking voices taunting him with their futility. How long he sat there brooding, he didn't know; his despair couldn't be measured in time.

More than once he'd entertained the idea that talking to someone might relieve his frustration and even provide him with alternative options. But the question always was, "To whom?" He couldn't confide in the servants; they'd be filled with fear. Curtis, his clerk? No. No point in worrying him. And Rosamund? How could he tell his daughter that their enemy, the arrogant Lord Frederick, had sent his manager to demand marriage to her as the price for peace? What he couldn't figure out was how the scoundrel even knew he had a daughter. No, Rosamund must not be told; she might consider it her duty to sacrifice herself for his sake.

Lord Schmidden gripped the lion's paws at the ends of his chair arms until the veins stood out like cords on the backs of his large hands. He bowed his head and his frown joined his brows above his nose. Surely, if he thought hard enough, he would find a pathway through this dilemma.

"I must find a way," he insisted, hammering a clenched fist on the broad chair arm. His words bounced off the stone walls and echoed like the relentless thoughts pounding the halls in his troubled mind. Then, slowly, the echoes faded back into silence.

When the uncanny sense of another's presence suddenly interrupted his torment and silenced the jeering voices, Lord Schmidden raised head, feverishly scrutinizing the room's darkest corners.

But there was no one there; he was alone.

Still the awareness persisted, beckoning to him from the gloom. Was it a mere shadow? Or perhaps a moonbeam? Maybe it was his imagination. Maybe it was . . .

His desperation overcame his long-nursed pride. "God?"

A log shifted in the fireplace and the charred coals burst into spiking flames. Lord Schmidden leaped from his chair. He didn't know how it happened, but suddenly he had a plan, an idea—a solution that restored his hope. As his mind raced with his thoughts, he lifted his hands in honest surrender and turned his face heavenward.

"Thank you, God!"

* * *

Even though she slept past her normal rising time, Rosamund awoke from her nightmare feeling agitated and irritable. She hurried through her morning ablutions and lifted a burning candle from a hallway sconce to light her way as she headed for the music room, her favorite refuge. Shielding the flame with her free hand, she picked up her pace as she crossed the great room's marble floor. Drapery panels hid the alcove, and Rosamund slipped between them, not bothering to swag them into the hooks on either side of the opening.

The lovely space, suitable for a cozy *tête-à-tête* or secluded practice, held two armless side chairs, their seats padded with green cushions. A low table displaying an empty brass candle holder and a local Bohemian-blown glass bowl filled with dried lavender buds filled the space between the chairs.

Inhaling the soothing aroma, Rosamund lit the tapers in the tall, ornate candle stand positioned strategically behind the harpsichord with the candle she'd carried with her. When light filled the room, she pressed her candle into the brass holder.

Fond of parties, dramas, and musicales, Rosamund's now-deceased grandmother, Lady Clara, had decided that the room, originally a storage compartment, would be remodeled to facilitate entertainments, and the space was large enough to accommodate a small group of musicians if the furnishings were removed.

The rose-colored marble panels masking the fieldstone walls were not only beautiful but reflected sound as well. A mosaic sunburst of small imported

Italian tiles in lapis blue, sun yellow, grass green, and cherry red paved the floor, and the several months it had taken a skilled craftsman to set them in place had proved time well spent.

Lord Schmidden had purchased a harpsichord, a relatively new invention, for Rose, his young English wife, soon after they were married, and the harp-shaped keyboard instrument stood at the center of the sunburst. Monsieur Pierre Monet, a traveling French musician, had remained at Burg Mosel for well over a year as Lady Rose's music instructor. Following Monsieur Monet's decision to move on, he had returned for a visit on several occasions, always claiming a desire to check up on his talented pupil.

After Lady Rose's mysterious disappearance during the festivities celebrating her husband's cousin's wedding, the instrument sat neglected. But one day when young Rosamund was just five years old, her father found her perched on the tall bench that he'd fashioned for his wife. Even though her legs swung short of the floor, she was eagerly trying to express the melodies she could hear in her head.

When Lord Schmidden peeked between the draperies, his pain at seeing anyone sitting in Rose's place was quickly replaced by delight when he heard the little tune his daughter had composed. After a few minutes he slipped quietly away and kept her secret until the time came to find someone to educate her, and then he chose an older widow with musical training. Frau Meta recognized the innate talent in her new charge and deliberately encouraged both lessons and creativity.

As time passed, music provided a constructive release for Rosamund's artistic energy and sometimes-desperate adolescent emotions, especially during the long, lonely winter days when she'd finished her lessons, Kathe was completing tasks in the scullery, and Papa was occupied with overseeing the villages on his land or away on a trip to some foreign place.

Numerous times she'd begged to accompany him, longing to see London, her mother's home, but he'd always insisted that traveling wasn't safe for pretty little girls, so she'd had to be content with his stories and gifts—and her music.

Today Rosamund slid onto the bench and placed her hands in playing position. Forcing her fingers to labor through one melancholy selection after another, she pounded out her frustration. Finally, the discord of keys crashing under fingers that had lost their way brought an end to her tortured music. She closed her eyes and dropped her head, resting her forehead on the instrument.

As the shrill dissonance faded, her father's approaching footsteps captured her attention. Her head came up. In the next moment, Lord Schmidden parted the curtains and entered the alcove wearing the smells of horse sweat and oiled leather, and she knew he'd been out riding.

Taking one look at him this morning, standing straight and confident, she never would have guessed the desperation he'd expressed such a short time ago. Despite her rush of affection, Rosamund couldn't muster her usual smile and distress put an edge in her greeting.

"Hi, Papa. What brings you here this time of day?"

He tweaked a curl that had escaped the satin-banded mesh *crespine* confining her hair and smiled indulgently. "Came to see my favorite girl."

She made her lips curve up but the smile didn't reach her eyes. "You're sweet, Papa."

"In truth, I'm here because I've got a plan." Rosamund stared at him suspiciously; he even sounded like his old self, bold and fearless.

"I know you won't like my idea. I didn't myself—at first." He paused when she braced her hands on the bench; then in the next breath he rushed his appeal, "But my plan is for the best, so please, listen to your wise, old papa."

Rosamund raised her brows. "All right, Papa. I'm listening." She moved her hands to her lap, but she couldn't help lacing and unlacing her fingers.

"It's not safe for you here if Lord Frederick follows through on his threat to attack us, so I want you to go stay with Edith, my old nurse who lives in Altwarp. No one would think to look for you in an old woman's hut in a fishing village that isn't even on my property. I'll get help to settle things with Lord Frederick. Then, when it's safe, I'll come get you."

Before he finished speaking, the bench legs scraped across the tile floor as Rosamund leaped to her feet. "Do you really think for a single minute that I'll leave you, Papa?" Her voice faltered with emotion, "Don't you *want* me here with you?" Her fierce eyes searched his face.

"You know I want you here, Rosamund," he protested sharply, "but I'll worry a lot less if I know you're safe." His Adam's apple bobbed as he swallowed and his voice came out sounding like tumbling gravel, "I couldn't bear it if anything happened to you."

Rosamund's chin tightened stubbornly. Her father was the thread that tied her whole life together. How could she ever choose to leave him?

When he reached up and wiped his hand over his face, she suddenly realized he'd already faced that decision and had determined to do what would be best for her. Now she must make a choice. And somehow it came to her that this decision marked her final step in becoming an adult.

January - 1423

## CHAPTER FOUR

The shabby gray wool cloak and ratty fur muff borrowed from Kathe to disguise her noble identity were no match for the icy shivers that darted down Rosamund's spine, and fear that she might never see her home or her father again filled her mouth with the dryness of stable straw. As her blue eyes followed the curving beams to the apex in Burg Mosel's vaulted entrance hall, she swayed on her feet; today the dizzying height left her feeling young and insignificant.

She clutched the marble stairway's newel post with cold fingers and dropped her worried gaze to her ancestors' painted-on-canvas faces in their gilt-edged frames that lined the mahogany paneled walls. Her chin stiffened as she glared at their glowering images. "What choice do I have?" she defied their disapproval with more sorrow than anger.

In the next moment, Lord Schmidden emerged

from the great room and advanced toward her along the corridor, his wood-soled shoes beating a foreboding rhythm against the marble floor. Rosamund swallowed the lump that rose in her throat and whirled around to face her father, expecting a warm hug—his customary greeting and farewell, but she immediately halted in her anticipation. Her father's eyes were down, his sole focus the small painted chest he carried in his hands.

Disappointment tightened her lips while her arms, raised to share their expected embrace, fell limply to her side. But before she had time to wonder about the small chest, he deposited the container on her waiting trunk and reached for the bell cord, tugging vigorously to summon Josef, the liveryman. Then he turned to her, his pre-occupation with the chest replaced by a look so intense that it burned away her momentary disappointment.

When he gathered her close in a tight hug, she wrapped her arms around him and rested her cheek against his broad chest. The familiar scent of his soap and leather nearly crumbled her already shaken composure, but she choked back her sobs in a determined effort to be brave.

Lord Schmidden finally pulled away—just far enough to see his daughter's face. He lifted her chin, met her brimming eyes with his own suspiciously damp gaze, and said gruffly, "I'll miss you fiercely, Rosamund, but it means everything to me to know you're safe. Always remember who you are, but don't reveal our situation to anyone, not even Edith. I've sent for help, and I'll come for you as soon as I can—by summer, I hope." He planted a firm kiss on each cheek, then abruptly released her and directed his attention to the colorful container, the cause of her dismay.

"I'm sending this little chest with you for safekeeping." His restless fingertips thrummed the painted lid. "It was your mama's wedding chest. I've always meant for you to have it, and this seems like the right time to give it to you. If anything should happen . . ." His gravelly voice broke, and his drumming fingers flattened tensely on the lid, as if to push away the truth that their present circumstances were beyond his control.

A blast of cold air swirled around them when the iron-braced oak doors swung open. Josef's slight cough, followed by his announcement, "Your ride is waiting, my lady," moved them to action; they turned together toward the outside world.

Staring out at the falling snow, Rosamund tried to suppress a terrified shudder. She was leaving her home. Perhaps forever. She bit her lower lip between her teeth to stop its quivering. So many times she'd wished to travel, to see the big world Papa had so vividly described.

But not like this.

Not alone.

While Josef deposited her trunk and the little chest on the sleigh floor, Rosamund clutched her father's arm and blinked back her tears. There was no changing her mind now. Side-by-side, they descended the broad stone steps to the sleigh waiting below on the snow-covered drive.

Her father steadied her until she was settled on the bench. She buried both hands in the scullery maid's ratty muff and sniffed in his familiar scent as he tucked a heavy bearskin rug around her. Growling a gruff goodbye, he stepped back and slapped the sleigh's side panel to signal the driver they should be on their way. When the sleigh pulled away with a jerk that mimicked the wrenching in her heart, Rosamund pulled one hand free to wave as she twisted around to watch Papa wave back.

As the distance widened between them, her self control came undone; the tears she'd held back while saying goodbye  gushed freely, blinding her eyes so she could hardly see him.

January 1423. Altwarp, Pomerania

## CHAPTER TWO

The air smelled of snow but the frozen ground was still bald. Trees held up naked arms as though begging God for winter coats, and smoke spires rose like prayers from the cluster of chimneyed dwellings. For weeks the villagers had talked of little else but the unusual winter.

That is, everyone except shriveled old Edith Baer. Mama Bear, as the villagers had affectionately nicknamed Edith, had scurried about with scarcely suppressed excitement while her friends shook their heads and asked among themselves, *Did Edith have some illness that was causing her to sip the medicinal spirits she urged on the village sick and weary?*

But no, Edith's bracing tonic still perched complacently on the widest of several stone ledges sticking out of her fireplace. In fact, she'd lifted the bottle down from its roost just the day before, but only to give it a quick dusting along with everything else in her humble home—the last of the two dozen or so wood and stone structures huddled along the coastline where rows of herring fence posts, sticking up like the protruding hairpins around her hair bun, marked the small fishing village nestled at the mouth of an inlet on the Baltic Sea coast.

Edith was not sick—but she did have a secret: she was expecting a guest. She knew that within a few days of Rosamund's arrival, her young guest would replace the unseasonable weather as the main topic of village gossip, and she knew she would enjoy every bit of the attention. But the anticipation of Rosamund's visit was her own sweet elixir, and her giddiness betrayed her.

As darkness descended, Edith welcomed her young guest with open arms and a hearty meal. While the two women sat near the fire, enjoying the cabbage, carrot, and rabbit stew that had simmered all day in a soot-blackened pot suspended over the fire, impatient pounding rattled Edith's crude wooden door. The old woman heaved her arthritic body onto her feet and shuffled across the room.

When Edith had lifted the heavy bar and scraped open the door, Rosamund started in fear at the sturdy male figure looming in the doorway. Had her father's enemy discovered her whereabouts so soon?

"Radmilla sent me to fetch you," the burly, bearded fellow addressed Edith in his rumbling bass. "The children are sick with the croup."

His sharp eyes, darting beyond Edith to settle on her guest, narrowed with curiosity mingled with suspicion, but he made no reference to Rosamund and merely delivered his request: "Come when you've finished eating."

Assuring him that she would be on her way shortly, Edith closed the door and dropped the cross bar into place with a thud. "Emil Buress, my neighbor, he is," she explained in the local vernacular she'd grown up speaking.

In a hasty effort to still her shaking hands and hide her shallow, rapid breathing from her elderly hostess, Rosamund jumped to her feet and began tidying the remains of their meal.

Unaware of her guest's distress, the old woman thanked Rosamund as she bundled up in a well-worn hooded fur coat that swept the ground with its sagging hem. She thrust her feet into weathered boots and pushed her wrinkled, brown-spotted hands into a pair of well-worn fur-lined leather gloves.

Dressed to face the cold, Edith grabbed her herb bag from the peg in the wall that was close to the door, slung the strap over her head, and turned back, speaking over her shoulder, "Be droppin' the bar when I'm gone, *Liebling*. Be back soon I will. Be puttin' more wood on the fire iffen ye will. I'll be knockin' when I come so's ye can enter me." She stepped over the threshold and heaved her shoulder against the moisture-swollen door until it groaned shut.

When the door had closed out Edith and the cold, Rosamund took advantage of her solitude to survey the earthy little cottage that was now her home. She plopped down on the rough bench, the room's only seating, and wondered if pinching herself would wake her from this frightful nightmare. But no, Edith's cottage seemed real enough. And so did the itchy *cotte,* one of several she'd borrowed from Kathe.

She hugged her arms around her middle and studied the walls of the hut. Brown and gray field stones stacked on top of each other were held together by gray mortar. A closer look revealed signs of disintegration; hollows pocked the mortar where fine gray powder had sifted to the floor below and stood in miniature mountains around the wall's bottom edges. Wooden beams and strips of lathe formed the upper walls, and dried mud bristling with bits of straw chinked in the cracks. The hard-packed dirt floor had been scraped so many times that it was now a step lower than the doorsill.

The fireplace grew out of the lower stone wall. Small bottles and crockery pots in assorted colors, shapes, and sizes lined the ledges formed by protruding stones. Several faded garments, two animal traps, and three handled pails hung on random wood pegs sticking out of the left wall. Two woven baskets sat below the pails—one held apples, parsnips, and wild carrots; the other was heaped with walnuts waiting to be shelled.

Rosamund eyed the patched brown duvet covering the straw tick bed in the far corner and shuddered at the prospect of sleeping on the floor. What if there were mice? Or rats? Even at Feste Burg, the Schmidden's fortress located farther up the Pomeranian coast, bed frames suspended sleepers off the floor. She swallowed a sob and told herself she should be thankful there were no chickens or goats living in Edith's house to host fleas and create stench and squalor.

The firelight playing peek-a-boo in the rafters drew her attention to the bundles of dried plants dangling from the rough ceiling beams. Tipping back her head and rolling her eyes, she straightened up from a disgruntled slouch. When the crude bench rocked back and forth, Rosamund jumped to her feet and impatiently grabbed one end, but scooting it forward made no difference, and further examination revealed that the legs were uneven.

Rosamund's rapid gaze scanned the hut. Spying a loose chunk of bark near the woodpile beside the hearth, she scooped it up and fitted it under the short end of the bench. When the seat was finally steady, she shrugged her shoulders and sat down, certain that stabilizing the bench would prove one of the simpler challenges she'd face while living in this primitive place.

As she looked around, her glance fell on her mother's wedding chest that Papa had sent with her. Impulsively crossing the room, she knelt on the straw covering the floor to examine the decorated container. In a tangible way this small chest represented her mother. She touched the lid with her index finger and then slowly traced the outlines of the colorful Annunciation figures depicted on the surface: the Angel Gabriel making his proclamation to the Virgin Mary.

Rosamund slid her hand along the chest's front and pressed the tiny button at the center. When she heard the catch click free, she raised the lid until it rested on its hinges.

As her hesitant fingers smoothed the purple silk lining, she caught a whiff of the faintly sweet, musky scent emanating from the treasure box. The aroma triggered a memory, and for a moment the door to the past cracked open: *I saw this chest on Mama's dressing table the night of Cousin Josie's wedding . . . I sat on a stool and watched her brush her long, dark hair.*

She squeezed one hand tightly in the other and pressed her lips together, mustering the courage to pick up the tiny wooden box resting loosely on top of the chest's bulkier contents. Her shaking fingers turned the container over and over as she suddenly found herself reluctant to disturb the past. Over the years, watching her friend Kathe interact with her mother, Rosamund had longed for her own mother—yet now she felt almost afraid of that intimacy.

Finally, steeling herself against her unexpected emotions, she applied pressure on the lid and gently slid it open along its grooves. The silence of Edith's cottage absorbed her awed gasp. A pair of dainty earrings nestled on a green velvet bed. A lustrous pearl adorned each gold ring and a second tear-shaped pearl dangled beneath it. As she lifted the earrings, the creamy pearls reflected the flickering firelight.

For an instant Rosamund was a little girl playing dress-up. She tossed back her cloud of dark curls and fastened the earrings into place on her ears. Nodding her head from side to side, the swaying pearls brushed her neck like a mother's tender kisses. She eased the lid into place on the small box and settled it on the floor by the chest. But she left the earrings on her ears to continue their whispery caress.

As eagerness to discover the chest's remaining treasures surged through her, Rosamund drew out a lumpy saffron-colored silk bag. When she'd loosened the drawstring cord, she turned the bag upside down and shook it. Three silver hairbrushes, their backs and handles mottled with tarnish, tumbled into her lap. Each back displayed an engraved scrolling *R* ... for Rose, her mother's given name. Glossy strands of long dark hair still clung to the stiff bristles, and she couldn't resist fingering them.

Selecting the smallest brush, she paused a moment and then impulsively ran it through her own dark hair. The sound of her own voice humming a long-forgotten lullaby surprised her. She stopped, hummed a few notes, and then continued through the melody a second time as she brushed her hair with lingering, rhythmic strokes.

The little lullaby and the gentle brushing evoked distant memories: Listening to bedtime stories. Walks in the rose garden. Sparkling jewels on gentle hands. A velvety skirt soft against her cheek. Memories as distant as her mother's elusive scent.

When the melody ended, slowly, pensively, she settled the brushes on the empty silk bag resting on the floor beside the earring box.

Her next discovery, a baby's baptismal gown and matching cap, elicited a soft "Ahh" when she examined the delicate stitches and wondered if her young mother had lovingly fashioned the little garments. She held up the cap and curled her left hand into the crown. With the fingers of her free hand she gently smoothed the long, silky ribbons. As she moved the cap this way and that by turning her wrist, her fist seemed to become a baby's wee head. And when she finally slipped the tiny headdress from her curled fingers and tenderly laid it aside, a wistful sigh warmed her lips.

She held up the dainty gown with its white-on-white embroidered bodice and shook out the long skirt's time-pressed folds. Her self-control relaxed along with the wrinkles; she clutched the little dress to her heart and whispered brokenly, "Mama, I was your little baby.

Bittersweet. Joy and pain. Finding, and losing all over again. A quick nod of her head sent her hot tears flashing away, but more slipped in to take their place. She smoothed the gown and cap with loving fingers. The fine linen felt as soft as a baby's skin. The sleeves weren't much bigger around than her thumbs. And were those tiny burgundy spots trailing along the hem perhaps the wine of celebration? What a joyous occasion it must have been. How happy her young parents, so looking forward to the future. Little did they know what it held for them.

And now, what did the future hold for her? Would love ever come to her? Would she one day be a mother? One day know the miracle of new life? A cloud of despair settled over her spirit. She was stuck in this primitive hovel—maybe forever—and her life held no promises.

Abruptly, she refolded the dainty garments and pushed away thoughts of her future as she returned her attention to the chest. She removed the final object. It was large and solid and wrapped in a watered-silk blue scarf. Another wooden box, perhaps?

As the luxurious fabric slipped off the object and draped across her lap, Rosamund's sharp exclamation filled the room. The treasure she held in her hands was not a box, it was a book—a rare possession indeed.

A large oval ruby set in gold filigree and surrounded by delicately etched vines and flowers adorned the hand-tooled ivory top panel. A small pearl formed the center of each flower. Impulsively, she touched each one, counting twenty-four in all. Gold filigree corner protectors added beauty and strength to the top and bottom panels, a bevel-edged ivory strip covered the spine that was secured by a leather binding, and the wide, ornate clasp beckoned with the allure of a secret waiting to be discovered. It was a Book of Hours, a nun's prayer book or a nobleman's wedding gift to his bride.

With her heart pounding in her fingers, Rosamund carefully unfastened the latch and opened the heavy cover. A pressed yellow rose slid out and nestled among the scarf's silken folds. She retrieved the papery flower and wondered at its significance. Oh, she did hope the book would give her a clue.

She laid the flower safely to one side and returned her attention to the book. As she turned the first page, she encountered the gilt-edged parchment presentation page. Startling words in her father's familiar handwriting leaped up at her:

*To my Bride, the most fragrant Rose in the Garden. With Fondest Affection, Nicklaus Schmidden.*

As she stared at her father's romantic

dedication, one thought filled her mind: *Was this cherished flower a wedding rose—her mother's wedding rose?*

She'd always considered the loss of her mother in personal terms, but she suddenly saw that her father's sorrow had been far greater than her own. She didn't even remember her mother. But Papa! He knew what he'd lost—and yet his love for her, their daughter, had given him the strength and courage to put her needs before his own.

She closed her eyes and sucked in a ragged breath. Instead of feeling sorry for herself, separated from her father and exiled to a primitive hut, Rosamund determined to follow her father's example, to think about other's needs above her own. And she would do it cheerfully, too—just like Papa.

Further examination of the book revealed that each handwritten page contained a passage from the book of Psalms, one for each hour in a day. Each *i* was dotted precisely and the curls on the stems of every *y* and *g* and *j* matched perfectly. Colorful cherubs, delicate flowers, and trailing vines illuminated the pages. Finely drawn tracery bordered each page. The book was an exquisite work of art.

A calendar indicating the Church's annual feast days followed the twenty-four readings, and a final page recorded a prayer, handwritten by the scribe himself. She read the words slowly.

*Lord, send the blessing of Thy Holy Spirit upon this book, that it may mercifully enlighten our hearts and give us a true understanding, and grant that by its teaching it may brightly preserve and make full abundance of good works according to Thy will. Amen.*

Rosamund closed her eyes on a fresh rush of emotion—and not just for the loss of her mother, nor for the beauty and heartbreak of her parents' love. She felt overwhelmed by the meaning of the prayer and the emptiness of her lonely heart that yearned for something she couldn't identify.

Until several weeks ago, her father had never mentioned God to her. And God was not referred to by the servants—not even her governess had spoken to her about God. Rosamund's vague idea of religion was based on a single childhood visit to the deserted and now-barred Chapel of the Shepherd at Burg Mosel.

As a five-year-old-girl, she'd sat on a hard bench

in the gloomy sanctuary and stared at the stained glass Shepherd holding a small white lamb. The Shepherd's kind eyes had evoked a strangely breathless feeling, which she'd convinced herself was just her imagination, never recognizing her soul's longing to know God.

When she lowered the book to rest on her lap, it fell open near the center to a portion of Psalm Sixty-three under the heading *Hour Twelve*:

*O God, thou art my God; Early will I seek thee,*
*My soul thirsteth for thee, My flesh longeth for*
*thee in a dry and thirsty land, Where no water is.*

"That's me!" Rosamund's startled whisper was absorbed by the crackling of Edith's fire.

*To see thy power and thy glory,*
*So as I have seen thee in the sanctuary.*

Again she experienced the same breathless sensation she'd felt as a child gazing at the Shepherd in the chapel window. Eagerly, she read on:

*Because thy lovingkindess is better than life,*
*My lips shall praise thee.*

The mysterious sense of warmth grew stronger.

Like a blanket, it enveloped her, soaking up the pain and loneliness and comforting her aching soul.

She dropped her head and closed her eyes, echoing the words of the psalm as she whispered her first prayer, "God, my soul is thirsty for You."

A sharp knock on the crude door disturbed the holy moment. Quickly closing the book, Rosamund slid it onto the silk scarf and rushed to the door, eagerly expecting to find Edith's plump figure waiting on the other side. Smiling, and warm to core of her heart, Rosamund raised the heavy bar and opened the door.

Her joyful welcome froze in her throat.

January 1423. Scania, Southern tip of Sweden

## CHAPTER THREE

It was the first week of the new year—and still there was no snow. Every winter the northern regions of the Baltic Sea would freeze, and although warm easterly winds and the low salt content due to the many fresh-water tributaries emptying into it kept the southern waters navigable, frequent storms blew through without warning, making maritime travel a death wish. But this year the anticipated mild winds had been strangely silent. Instead, cold arctic air had swept down from the north and the entire sea was now blanketed with an unprecedented coating of thick ice.

Pale sunlight filtered through the bare tree branches like the fingers of God, briefly stroking the frozen world below. Crisp ground crunched under Captain Erik Branden's feet as he stomped toward the coast, where his flat-bottomed, high-sided oak cog lay anchored.

Erik lifted his face to the sun, an invitation to its thin rays to warm his ruddy, wind-roughened cheeks. His blond hair that mingled with the red-gold fox fur edging his hood caught the light and formed a halo around his face.

But the sunshine did nothing to soothe Erik Branden's inner turmoil. Lord Schmidden's urgent request for help, waiting for him when he'd arrived in Scania, presented a problem he didn't know how to solve, and the longer he considered his dilemma, the greater his struggle.

Seven summers past, when solstice winds had blown Erik and his crew of seamen and soldiers off course and damaged the main sail and rigging on The Tarragon, Lord Schmidden had provided food and shelter for them all at Feste Burg. Erik had promised to return the favor if Lord Schmidden should ever need his help—and had the nobleman's request come at any other time, Erik would have immediately set out to help his friend. But he and his crew, at great risk, had returned to Scania only two days ago from what had proved to be a long and difficult expedition to Riga, Livonia. Located at the mouth of the Daugava River, Riga marked the northerly end of one of the European Hansa trade routes.

On the return trip, Erik always made the stop in Scania to reunite several crew members with their families, but he never wintered there, preferring instead to spend the off season at the continental port city of Lübeck, nick-named "Queen of the Hanseatic League," where repairs could be made to The Tarragon and several members of his crew annually sponsored a booth in the *Christkindlmarket* to sell their wood carvings, results of a favored hobby while they were at sea. However, this year's unusual arctic winds and unprecedented freeze had trapped them on the north side of the Baltic.

Erik shook his head in frustration. Cold water was one thing, ice was quite another. Prolonged exposure to the freezing temperatures would cause The Tarragon's wooden planks to shrink and the joints to pull apart, and it would require months of hard work to make the vessel seaworthy again.

His other option, to march his crew around the sea, would take far too long. Besides, overdue snow could come any day to hamper or halt ground travel until spring. He knew they would reach the continent sooner if they waited for the ice to thaw.

But this end of his personal resourcefulness was the hardest thing he'd ever faced. Two things he dreaded: to quit and to fail. A very capable person, Erik was rarely at a loss for an answer, a decision, a solution. His unusual insight and instinct, even in his youth, had brought about his promotion from crew member to captain, and his men risked their lives based on his decisions.

For twelve years Erik had lived on the sea, a carrier of goods, customs, and social change. And although many of his contemporaries had eventually married and settled down to agrarian life, Erik still roved the sea, restlessly pursuing adventure as he transported grain, textiles, furs, fish, amber, honey, and salt—two hundred tons per load—for the Hanseatic League, an affiliation of merchants throughout northern Europe committed to protecting commerce and trade from bandits and thieves.

Now twenty-eight, a decade past the normal marrying age for men, Erik struggled with a deep inner ache. He longed for a home and a family of his own.

His quest for freedom and knowledge of the world had driven him to the sea as a youth, but two years ago, Svenn, a Norwegian fisherman, had shared with him the reality of personal communication with God and the assurance of salvation through Jesus Christ. Erik had opened his heart and experienced a spiritual awakening. And that new awareness had been accompanied by a desire for a wife who would share his faith, not just his kitchen and his bed.

Although the demands of his many expeditions had prevented him from developing an intimate relationship with anyone, the longing continued to grow. Today, his hidden yearning ruptured into agony as he wrestled with himself. Should he put aside his personal desire and start planning a spring expedition, with the hope that he would arrive in time to help his friend? Was God asking him to take up a cross of duty to a friendship? Did God understand how rootless and lonely he felt? Could God indeed be trusted with his future?

The timing of Lord Schmidden's request, the distance around the sea, and Erik's own deep yearning for a wife all compounded his frustration over the unusual weather. He weighed his options, arguing with himself. To go back on his word was unthinkable; it violated his conscience. Yet, unless he could walk on water . . .

Aggravated at such a cynical thought, he stomped his boot-clad feet. Then slapping his mitted hands together, he burst out, "Fantasy isn't faith, Erik. No one walks on water!"

Looking up from the frosted coast where stiff spikes of frozen grass reminded him of the steel needles he used to mend his sails, Erik put his hand to his forehead to shield his eyes from the glare of the winter sun reflecting off the hard-crusted snow. He studied his seaworthy cog's brightly painted dragon's head carved into the prow. He'd chosen the vessel for its workmanship, but the masthead, salvaged from a long-abandoned Viking ship, symbolized his invincibility.

As he stared at The Tarragon, he realized that this agent of his self-reliance was held firmly captive by a sea of ice that would not be melting anytime soon. He was trapped. For how long, he didn't know. Frustration at his powerlessness overwhelmed him.

He stepped onto the frozen sea and moved close to the masthead. With his mitted palm he stroked the weathered carving that had always been a source of inspiration—but the strength of its power was now reduced to human terms. He wrapped his hand around the prow's curved beam and pressed his forehead against the cold wood. As he closed his eyes he wished he could shut out the reality that his world had come to an icy end; his ship was more useless than the toy boats his father had carved for him when he was a boy.

"God," his cry erupted from the depths of his being, "help me understand Your purpose."

When Erik finally raised his head and cast his agonized gaze up at the great symbol of his former strength, a strange thought brushed against the fringe of his mind.

*God certainly has me immobilized. Could it be that He is trying to redirect my life?*

Erik shrugged to dismiss the fleeting thought, but as his glance shifted downward from the masthead to his feet standing firmly on the ice, a radical idea exploded in his mind. His body burned with daring and fear and his breath came in sharp gasps. Every sea-hardened muscle tensed. Like breakers crashing against a cliff, his thoughts peaked and plummeted until his whole body dripped with sweat—like spray in the wake of his revelation.

The answer was right in front of him.

Beneath his very feet.

He *could* walk on water. Frozen water!

* * *

Erik's outrageous proposal captured his crew's imagination. As excited as schoolboys, the men pooled their resources. Crew member Olaf and his wife Inga offered their cabin for meetings and as the storehouse for accumulating supplies.

Within a matter of days, eight lightweight sleds stood upright against the end wall of the cabin. Getelds, A-frame rectangular tents made of animal skins, were folded and stacked at one end of the main room, and the supporting poles leaned against the end of the house beside the waiting sleds. The crew of twenty-four spent one whole day practicing "set up" and "take down" to insure the process for providing shelter could be accomplished quickly and smoothly, even in the dark.

Each man supplied a sword, two boiled wool blankets for sleeping, a hooded fur coat, leather leggings, and mitts and boots lined with a thick layer of rabbit down to provide insulation against the cold and ice. Soliciting dried fish and game from local villagers, friends, and relatives provoked various reactions—folks responded with every emotion from envy or encouragement to scorn and skepticism. But nothing dampened the men's enthusiasm.

In spite of the gossip and derision, Erik moved ahead with confidence; he'd never been so sure of anything. When he'd reached the end of his own resourcefulness, only God had remained dependable. And even though his crew members thought they knew their leader well, suddenly it seemed they didn't know him at all. His conviction, quite different from his former bold daring, inspired them with extraordinary determination.

On the day Erik and his crew planned to depart, the sun broke through a week-long cloud cover. Its shining rays transformed the frost-covered trees and blades of grass into a wonderland of glistening crystal prisms. The crew of twenty-four men gathered at the wharf, their spirits at peak excitement. They burst out in jolly chanting, "Heave ho, set it low. Heave ho, let it go. Heave ho, here we go. Heave ho, let it snow." Erik grinned at their buoyant enthusiasm, but his heart sensed God smiling at them through His creation.

The eight sleds bulged with blankets, food, firewood, and two large cauldrons. Even though the fierce cold sucked life from everything it touched, family members and local villagers, including old men who wished they were young enough to join the expedition, came to see them off on their adventure. This would be a story to tell the grandchildren.

Erik reviewed basic instructions with his men. "We'll eat on the move. Do you have today's provisions?" He waited for a nod from each crew member before continuing. "Daylight is short this time of year, so we won't stop until dark. It will be your responsibility to catch up after you step aside to relieve yourself. Stay alert; it's impossible to anticipate every danger. All right, any questions?" He looked around. "No? Then assume your stations."

The crew set off, resembling furry bears more than toughened seamen and soldiers. If all went as planned, it would take two full days of hard walking to reach Europe's northern coast. Erik thought they were not unlike Moses and the Israelites for whom God parted the Red Sea so they could cross on dry ground. God had spread out a pathway for them: forty-five miles of ice.

Initially they set a rapid pace. The ice along the coast was thick and land was still in view. Jagged peaks of distant mountains formed black silhouettes against the vast blue sky. Patches of bare ice reflected the sun's blinding glare. As late morning became midday, conversation ebbed and flowed like the rising and falling of the tide. The adrenaline of adventure bubbled in their veins. Courage and excitement soared in the cold, clear air, and they laughed and joked the way men do in the camaraderie of risk.

As they neared Bornholm, an island covered with spruce trees, they could see animal tracks in the fine frost covering the ice. Rabbit. Bird. Deer. Footprints of the creatures that made the island their home. And mingled with their marks of passing, Erik observed his own footprints, different in size and shape, yet nevertheless proclaiming that he, too, had been there and left an impact.

The afternoon sun sank in the sky, gradually embracing the horizon, and the thick-ribbed ice gave way to a smooth, shining gloss. Erik noticed that the men had grown quiet and their pace had assumed the meter of marching steps.

Thud. Thud. Thud. Thud. Their rhythmic footsteps pounded the ice.

When they approached the area where Erik estimated that the south and west underwater currents intersected, he opened his mouth to alert them to the possibility of thin ice. But before he could speak he was interrupted by a sudden, loud bang, a sharp thunderclap that rent the air. The crew members with free hands slapped them over their ears while those grasping sled ropes tried to duck their heads between their shoulders like neck-retracting turtles.

The ensuing silence was so brief no one had time to recover before another deafening crash pierced the air.

And then another.

The disabling sounds seemed to originate with their feet and shoot out in all directions.

Horror surged through Eric when he realized that the ice beneath them had indeed cracked and a large section was already sinking into blue-black water. “Disperse!” he shouted. “Move left!”

His men scrambled to reach safe ice, but those closest to the growing hole could not find secure footing and began slipping toward certain death. Panting and heaving, the crew members nearest to them reached out and jerked them to safety.

The ice continued to snap, crackle, and rumble, sending shudders through the crew as they watched rushing black water swell up to cover the spot where they'd been standing only moments before. No one said a word. The danger of their undertaking had suddenly become very real.

Commanding the men to regroup, Erik advised them to maintain individual pacing as a precautionary measure. And even though the ice proved solid from that point on, Erik decided he would be wise to cut short their sleep time; they would continue walking longer than he'd planned. *The less time we spend on the ice, the greater the chance we'll all survive,* he said to himself.

As they progressed toward the continent, the smooth, glassy surface of the ice became rough and cratered, and even though the men were weathered and hearty, they began to grow weary. The bouncing sleds generated an irritating racket, and the fading daylight made it difficult to see the frozen wind ridges that ruffled the ice; several men stumbled and almost fell.

Erik tried to lighten the mood with a little humor, telling a joke that sent laughter through the crew, distracting their thoughts from their aching backs and throbbing feet. They picked up their lagging pace and once again engaged in lively conversation. Several debated whether or not the sea had ever frozen solid in the past. No one could recall a grandfather or older friend or relative ever mentioning such an unusual occurrence.

The men fell silent as the sky grew dark and stars popped out, dotting the sky. When Olaf, bringing up the rear, thought he heard something moving behind him he slowly turned his head. Five pairs of eyes stared back at him. Gleaming eyes. Desperate eyes.

Although the smell of wild flesh burned his nostrils, he couldn't quite make out the shapes. But when one pair of eyes suddenly darted in closer, he got a good look at a full-grown gray wolf. And it was a thin wolf. A hungry wolf.

"Turn and defend when you hear the signal."

Olaf's hastily issued order jumped from man to man, instructing them to turn and attack when he whistled. The message was still moving among the crew when Olaf pursed his lips and produced a shrill whistle.

The men halted.

Turned and raised their swords.

Two lunging wolves were cut down mid-air. Two others backed into the shadows and began circling. Eyes gleaming and fangs bared, they snarled aggressively. A fifth wolf sniffed frantically at the limp, bleeding bodies of his fallen companions. When he raised his head and howled, the mournful, eerie cry sent shivers along Erik's veins.

The snarling pack regrouped and moved in for a second attack. Hackles raised, ears swept back, and tails upright, two lean, desperate shadows darted straight in with their heads down, aiming for the men's legs. When a third gray form shot in from the side in a powerful leap, Olaf plunged his sword into the beast's silvery winter coat. He thrust again and again, stabbing frantically, desperately.

Man and wolf, they fell together, arms and legs flailing.

The other two predators crouched, ready to

pounce on Olaf and his opponent. In that moment of panic no one knew whether the wolves meant to assist in the attack or take advantage of their partner's kill. However, Leif and Kjell put an end to the threat of such a tragedy. Leaping at the wolves from both sides, they brought their swords crashing down on the beasts' backs. Those standing closest heard the wolves' bones snap as their bodies slammed onto the ice.

Olaf rolled away from the still-twitching carcass of the wolf he'd just killed. He was not seriously injured, but when he tried to stand, his legs buckled and he started to shake. Karl retrieved a blanket from their supplies and wrapped it around Olaf's shoulders.

One. Two. Three. Four. Five. The wolves lay dead on the ice. They left them where they'd fallen, grisly shadows of death.

Progress resumed. And so did discussion. Each crew member had his own impression of what had just happened, and after the attack had been discussed from every angle, talk branched off into other daring adventure tales, including that of the revered hero, Beowulf.

Weary and isolated by the darkness, each crew member concentrated on placing one foot in front of the other. Discouragement pounced, almost as deadly as the wolf attack. Morning would never come. Land was nowhere to be found. They'd been foolhardy to make such a journey. Olaf had nearly been killed, to say nothing of those who'd almost drowned. They should never have listened to Erik. What had happened to their common sense? How could they have been so foolish?

Erik, aware of his men's despondency, was nevertheless determined to keep going until significant distance separated them from the dead wolves. He felt that distance would provide a measure of safety.

Finally, after what seemed like an endless trek, Erik called for a halt. The men shouted their relief and quickly set up camp.

Whale oil lanterns cast ghoulish, mocking shadows onto the ice as the crew laid out the tent poles: two crossed poles for each end of the rectangular A-frame structures. The men spread the tent skins over the poles, arranging them so the crossed ends protruded through holes in the skins.

With one man lifting each pole and four poles to a tent, they raised the skins and dropped the pole bottoms into the holes they'd chopped in the ice. Ridge poles were settled into the crotches made by the crossed poles. The completed shelters circled the sleds like sentries standing guard.

Before the men retired, Erik reminded them to sleep in their clothes on top of their blankets to insulate themselves from the ice. One crew member from each tent took the first watch while the remaining men settled for the night.

Erik moved quickly from tent to tent, checking on the men and speaking briefly with those on watch. When he felt certain everything was secure, he slipped into his own tent space and unrolled his blankets.

Stretched out on his back with his arms crossed behind his head, he looked up into the darkness. A few shining stars winked at him through the small gap around the tent poles. He'd always loved to watch the stars, to think of their well-ordered march across the sky, and in that instant he felt God's presence. A trusting smile turned up the corners of his mouth as he closed his eyes.

Shortly before daybreak the men on final watch woke the crew. Everyone rose quickly and bound up their blankets. While some men dismantled the shelters, others reloaded the sleds. A third group built a fire with kindling they'd brought along. They chopped out shallow chunks of ice and placed them in a large metal cauldron suspended over the fire on a tripod made of short poles brought along for that purpose; the melted ice would provide drinking water for the day.

When the men had satisfied their thirst and every item had been carefully repacked, the crew set off again. The novelty, however, had worn thinner than the dried venison strips they'd eaten for breakfast. The men lacked enthusiasm, and time seemed suspended.

Around noon a sharp wind began to blow in from the east. Dark clouds moved overhead and blotted out the pale winter sunlight. Dry crystals of loose ice whipped around them, stinging their noses, cheeks, and brows, and a dense fog settled in, impeding visibility. The combination of cold wind, flying ice particles, and swirling, damp fog stiffened their furs, making mobility a chore. Vapor from their breath turned to ice on their lashes and formed icicles that dripped from their beards. They trudged along for hours, miserable and weary. No one talked. By late afternoon the men resembled jerking marionettes controlled by an inexperienced manipulator.

When Kjell, in the lead, tripped over a frozen tuft of sedge sticking up through the ice, he fell, sprawling on the ice. He grabbed a handful of the stiff grass blades, rolled to his back, shot his arm in the air in a victory gesture, and bellowed one word: "Land!"

Even though the fog was so thick they couldn't see more than a few steps in front of them, the men's spirits soared. Their heavy feet grew suddenly fleet and they started running. When their boots finally crunched on solid ground, they hooted and yelled so loudly they should have cracked the ice—but no one cared. Land at last!

Light-headed and slightly dizzy, Erik closed his eyes. He'd never doubted the success of this endeavor, but the wonder of living minute by minute through a miracle reminded him of coming in from the cold: nose, ears, fingers, and toes all sting and tingle, and then one's whole body flushes with heat until every nerve comes alive. His inner being tingled with the awareness of God's presence. In response, he raised his hands in gratitude, acknowledging God's power.

Bordering on hysteria, the crew members boosted Erik to their shoulders and leaped around him, shouting in frenzied excitement.

By the time the men had calmed down and established camp, a northerly wind had driven away the fog. The crew eagerly welcomed sleep, but Erik, restless from the excitement, set off by himself. Tomorrow he and his men would begin the final leg of their journey and he would again have to consider the crew's welfare above his own needs—but tonight he craved time alone.

## CHAPTER FOUR

A fur-encased male figure filled the doorway, and a pair of eyes the blue of a Nordic sky gazed out from between frosted golden lashes. Shaken to her toes, Rosamund gasped and took an involuntary step back. The color came and went in her face as she stared at the Captain of the Tarragon; she would know Erik Branden anywhere.

For one breath-robbing second she was ten years old again, and he was her childhood hero. *He came back for me!* Her pulse leaped with elation. And then her mind spiraled with the prosaic thought that he wasn't as tall as she remembered. A tremor shook her body and she blinked, reconnecting with reality; seven years had passed since she'd last seen him—and of course, she had grown taller.

His deep, familiar voice startled her out of her stupor. "Good evening. I'm Captain Erik Branden. I walked around the point and meant to go back directly, but I came farther than I'd planned." He glanced past her, taking in the humble dwelling. "Would you allow me to rest by your fire?"

"U-uh," Rosamund stuttered, stepping aside so he could enter. "P-Pardon my rudeness; I was expecting someone else." As he moved past her, their eyes met, sending sudden tension through her limbs. Would he recognize her?

But he looked right through her and began removing his ushanka, followed by his heavy fur coat that wrapped his well-built form like a cocoon.

She stole covert glances at him while her mind raced. Were there medicinal herbs in Edith's stew that had altered her sense of reality? she wondered, reaching for wood to stoke the fire—anything to anchor her to reality. Could the disillusionment over Lord Frederick and the stress of their situation have caused her to hallucinate a visitation from the man she'd idolized?

Rich memories of the two weeks he and his crew had spent at Feste Burg flooded her mind. Memories of wading barefoot in shallow sea water. Laughing when he'd saved her from being struck by the falling boulder that showered them with icy spray. Collecting sea shells. Learning about the little creatures that had made those shells their home. Studying the stars and discovering she could identify the Hunter and the Crab, the Dippers, and the North Star. She knew she'd asked a thousand questions. Too many questions. But he'd always been patient with her. And somehow, he'd known all the answers.

He'd taken her aboard his ship and allowed her to watch from a safe distance while his men made repairs on the damaged sail and rigging. And he'd showed her the Portolan charts he used for navigating. He was a good teacher to an eager and adoring pupil.

Erik was her first male friend outside of her father, but his stay had passed all too quickly. When the repairs were completed, Erik and his crew said goodbye and set sail once again.

And no one knew that every spring Rosamund anxiously awaited the move to her family's summer residence, always harboring the secret hope that Erik would come back. And each year during their stay at Feste Burg she climbed the stairs to the top of the tower every morning to look out to sea, searching the horizon for a certain ship. But it never came. And after five years she finally put the memory away with other childhood treasures.

And now, he was here—in Edith's cottage!

She eyed him appraisingly. He had the same strong jaw and boyish smile, just as she remembered. Handsome, yes. But more than that, he had developed deeper strength in his face and greater breadth to his shoulders.

She felt suddenly overcome with an intense feeling of admiration and wonder; Erik Branden was touching her life a second time. And she would never be the same.

Rosamund put her hand to her throat to still the throbbing that left her breathless. But her mind was in utter confusion: How did he come to be here? He said he'd walked a long way and he was tired—and he was no doubt thirsty, as well.

"W-Would you like a hot drink?" she managed to inquire, and by the time he had settled on the bench, she handed him a steaming mug.

As he wrapped his hands around the warm drink, Erik eyed the open chest with its contents heaped on the floor beside it.

Noting that his gaze took in her treasures and then returned to the Book of Hours resting on the silk scarf, Rosamund suddenly recalled her father's warning to tell no one who she was or why she was living in Edith's cottage. Fear choked off her breath; did that include Captain Branden? How would she explain her father's signature in the book?

And what would she do with her heart if she discovered he was here to aid her father's enemy?

* * *

Erik cast a puzzled glance at the peasant girl. The firelight had turned her roughly woven *cotte* to velvet. Her eyes glistened and soft curls framed her face. But while her beauty was not lost on Erik, it was overshadowed by a nagging sense of familiarity that he couldn't readily identify. He shrugged to himself and turned his attention to her book.

Books were rare, and this one was obviously very special. How did this peasant girl, living in a hut in an insignificant fishing village, come to possess such a valuable book; a book that belonged in a castle or a convent?

Were this chest and its contents stolen?

Or was she not really a village girl . . . despite her

shabby clothing, her innate poise and startling beauty certainly seemed out of place in this hovel.

Well, there was one way to find out.

"Do you read?" he asked, deliberately keeping his eyes on the book; only the wealthy were educated.

She was so long in answering that he glanced up, catching a guarded expression on her face. And when their eyes met, she seemed to be struggling for composure, rubbing her palms nervously against the rough homespun covering her hips.

But as the connection went on, her shoulders relaxed and her lips gave him what seemed to be a mysterious half-smile that warmed her dark blue eyes with a tinge of violet, and he searched them with an intensity he'd never felt before.

"Yes, I read. And write." She motioned toward the book, "It's a collection of Psalms—from the Bible. About God." She raised her finely arched brows slightly and tipped her curly head. "And you. Do you read and write?"

Erik nodded, but this uncanny sense of connection was unsettling, to say the least. Why did he feel he should know her?

"May I?" He indicated the beautiful book in an effort to redirect his focus.

At her nod, he lifted the volume, settled it firmly on his knees, and opened the clasp. As the girl pushed his furs to the end of the bench and sat beside him, the faint scent of heather filled his nostrils. He couldn't help himself; he glanced at her again. She was so close, he could see the pulse beating in her throat.

Reluctantly, he tore his gaze away from her and focused on the ivory-covered book. The leather binding creaked when he lifted the heavy cover. With deliberate care, he turned to the presentation page. A pressed yellow rose slid out, and the girl quickly caught it with her slender fingers—he observed they were well cared for and without callouses, further confirming his guess that she didn't belong here. She held it in her lap, almost cradling it, as if it were . . . sacred.

He blinked to clear his mind of his peculiar thoughts and focused on the inscription.

"Nicklaus Schmidden!" The name shot out of his mouth like a blast from a battering ram. He whipped his head around, his brows pinching together as he studied the young woman again, more intently this time.

The sudden realization of her identity startled him. "Why, you're little Rosamund. Rosamund Schmidden." No wonder she seemed so familiar! "What are you doing here?" He pulled back and his voice sharpened, "Why aren't you with your father?"

Her eyes quickly became shuttered. "I live here."

Erik opened his mouth and then shut it. The finality of her reply was a reproof that forbade further probing. He looked down at the book in his hands, his mind spinning like a wooden top as he tried to balance the past with the present. What had he said to put her off? There were at least a dozen questions he wanted to ask. Questions about her father, about the threatened attack, about the summons for help, about why she was living here, about the years that had passed since he'd last seen her. But she'd made it obvious she didn't want him to ask. Or maybe she didn't know . . .

The ominous quiet that followed caused the hairs on the back of his neck to prickle.

When he finally lifted his head, Rosamund looked him straight in the eyes and broke the awkward silence, "And you. Why have you come here?"

As he shifted on the bench, his piercing gaze probed into her mind, indeed seemed to plunge into her very soul. "Your father sent for me. Didn't you know?" When she gasped and shook her head, he knew he'd taken her by surprise.

His fingers tightened on the book as he stared at her for a long minute. Merciful God in Heaven, she was the loveliest thing he'd ever seen!

His senses reeling, Erik continued to stare at her—and watched a slow flush brighten her cheeks. Her chest rose and fell with her soft, quick breaths, and her dark lashes dropping over her eyes didn't completely hide her sweet confusion.

Erik tore his glance away and redirected the conversation in an attempt to be diplomatic. "You said this is a book of Psalms—about God." This could prove a touchy subject as well, but she'd brought it up. And it was worth the risk. He focused on the book to give her personal space if his question made her uncomfortable, but to his satisfaction she answered immediately.

"Oh, yes." Her eyes flew to his and her words

held sheer joy. "I . . . felt His presence . . . when I read it."

"I understand," he said, returning her look without faltering.

The world of Edith's primitive cottage slipped into the shadows as Erik sensed Rosamund had forgiven him for questioning her presence in this hut that stood in such contrast to her station in life. But it was more than that for Erik; it was as if a curtain had been torn away. This lovely creature was the child he'd known, but her girlishness had disappeared and she was a woman now. A beautiful woman. Her long lashes shadowed the deep blue of her eyes. The beauty of her half-parted lips, the throbbing hollow at her throat, the soft roundness of her feminine shape ignited that heady scent, desire. To kiss her. To hold her in his arms. He smiled grimly to himself. And to think he'd wondered as the years passed if he was capable of such feelings.

His fingers tightened on the Book of Hours until his knuckles turned white and the blood pounded in his temples. What should he do with this kindredness of spirit that made him want to know her on every level? To know her in the warm shadows of this world and in the blinding glory of spiritual oneness. To merge the two realms into one.

*You're just being foolish,* he admonished himself sternly. *Your nerves are strained from the past month's preparations and the stress of crossing the sea on ice—and now discovering Lord Schmidden's daughter living in a fisherman's hut.*

He forced himself to redirect his thoughts, asking a question in what he hoped would pass for a normal voice. "So, tell me about your mother. I don't recall meeting her."

Rosamund shifted on the bench, her eyes wide and startled. "Papa never told you about her?"

He watched the changing expressions flow over her face and shook his head.

"I don't remember much about her." Her voice thinned to a strained thread. "She disappeared when I was only five."

"Disappeared?" Erik's dismay echoed in the word; he wondered if he'd heard correctly.

"Yes," Rosamund whispered, the pain creasing her face made him want to comfort her. But he hesitated, fearing he would frighten her. She confided apologetically, "It sounds unbelievable, I know. I suppose that's why we never talk about it." He noticed she'd clasped her hands together so tightly that her nails dug into her soft skin. "I can only tell you what I remember. Papa's cousin, Lady Josie, was getting married, so there was a lot of excitement at Burg Mosel."

Once she started to talk, Erik got the impression that thoughts and emotions she'd long held inside were bursting out, perhaps for the first time.

She stared into the fire as she reminisced. "I had a new blue *cotte*. And my first pair of dress-up gloves. They were made of white leather and had tiny pink rosebuds with green leaves embroidered on them."

She tipped her head slightly, as if replaying the events in her mind. As she did, her dark hair brushed Erik's shoulder, sending a shock rippling through him.

"Mama was so beautiful," Rosamund continued. "She wore a tiara in her hair. Papa called her his fairy queen," she smiled at the memory, "and he said I was his fairy princess."

Her voice softened. "I remember the singing. And the sweet smell of incense. And flickering candles that made the saints painted on the walls seem alive. There were guests, all dressed up. And Lady Josie looked so happy." She stared into the fire.

"After the wedding everyone enjoyed a party with music and dancing and wonderful food. Nurse gave me a piece of fruitcake and some hot cider. The cake tasted so good that I sneaked a second piece, but just then Nurse came to get me ready for bed, so I hid it behind my back."

She shifted on the bench. "The cake stained my new *cotte*, and nurse scolded me for being greedy; she said God would punish me. I didn't know who God was, but I felt so ashamed and afraid that I cried myself to sleep." Rosamund's lips trembled; obviously the memory was still painful, even after all these years.

"Later, Nurse told me the guests played games after I went to bed. During hide-and-seek, Mama went to hide. Several guests saw her go down the hall toward the chapel." Her breath came in a soft sob. "And that was the last time anyone ever saw her. Searching went on for days. But nobody found her. And she never came back."

Tears glistened on her lashes as she confided, "I thought it was my fault—that I was somehow being punished for being greedy." She hesitated, and then added, "But Papa blamed God; he's ignored God ever since." Reaching up with shaking fingers, she quickly whisked away her falling tears.

"F-forgive me for being so emotional," she whispered. "I've never told anyone these things." As if keeping her hands busy would alleviate her embarrassment, she lifted the rose from her lap and placed it back in the book.

Erik closed the Book of Hours, swallowing the lump in his throat as he fastened the clasp. He'd remained quiet while Rosamund talked, and now he found himself hoping that she, by sharing the feelings hidden in her heart for so many years, might be revealing the same desire to know and be known by him as he felt toward her. Abandoning caution, he reached out his hand to comfort her.

Loud pounding shook the door, interrupting them, and Rosamund immediately jumped up to answer the knock. Erik's hand dropped through empty space.

Rosamund wiped her eyes with the backs of her hands and cleared her throat as she crossed the room. With a firm tug she lifted the heavy bar and opened the door. And when she stepped back, Erik saw a hefty bearded fellow standing in the doorway. Placing the book on the bench, Erik rose to his feet.

Without waiting for an invitation, the visitor stooped and stepped inside. Shoving the door closed with a strong swing of his arm, he stomped the snow from his feet and demanded the brown stone crock of dried mustard stored on a fireplace ledge. "Edith needs it," was his terse explanation.

Immediately, Rosamund moved toward the fireplace, and the two men watched her as she reached up to retrieve the brown mustard pot from its perch.

Her slender, feminine figure moving about in a domestic setting triggered Erik's long suppressed hunger for a place of his own shared with someone special to make it a home. The flash of yearning that surged through him left him trembling.

When Rosamund turned toward Emil Buress with a warm smile and handed him the mustard pot, jealousy stabbed Erik in the heart. Did Rosamund's smile hold more than friendship? Who was this burly fellow, anyway? He seemed very at home in this cottage. Could Rosamund be his wife? And if so, was he good enough for her? Erik bit down hard on the inside of his cheek, causing the taste of warm blood to mingle with the saliva in his mouth.

"And who might this be?" Emil interrupted the awkward silence, jerking his ushanka-covered head toward Erik.

"This is m-my childhood friend, Erik Branden," Rosamund blushed and stammered out an explanation.

Emil shot Erik a piercing look and grunted, "Mind yourself," before he departed as abruptly as he'd come.

Red-faced, Rosamund shoved the door shut behind him and dropped the heavy bar. The loud bang as it fell into place jolted Erik out of his daze. He suddenly realized he'd forgotten the time.

"I must be going," he exclaimed, avoiding Rosamund's eyes for fear she would read in his the conflicted feelings that gripped him. He hurriedly donned his heavy furs, but he felt Rosamund watching him. And when he lifted his chin, their eyes met. Erik froze, speechless as a schoolboy. He could hardly breathe. And she seemed equally stunned.

They stared at each other for a long, suspended

moment before she blurted into the awkward silence, "It's snowing. I hope you don't have far to go." Her ordinary words bridged the uncomfortable gap between their emotional connection and the reality of his departure.

Erik cleared his throat and shook his head, trying to pretend nothing had happened between them. "No, not too far." He knew he had to go. But he desperately wanted to stay.

When he reached the door, he took her slender hand in his mitted grasp. "Good-bye, Rosamund. God keep you." He hesitated, as unsaid words hung between them. Squeezing her hand, he gave her a searching look that said too much—yet not nearly enough.

And then he was gone.

Outside in the snow, Erik took several steps before he turned to look back. Rosamund stood motionless in the doorway, her feminine shape a silhouette against the firelight. He raised his hand in farewell then lowered his head and faded into the kaleidoscope of softly falling snow. He was alone in the darkness with his soul-shaking discovery.

* * *

Rosamund shut out the pinching cold and sank to the floor beside the bench, limp as a rag doll without its stuffing.

"Erik Branden—here!" she whispered the exclamation under her breath. She hadn't thought of him in a long time. Years, in fact.

But the look in his eyes! She flushed again even though there was no one to see, rejoicing in the secret satisfaction that Erik no longer regarded her as a child.

And then her mind bombarded her with questions: Why didn't I ask him how he got here? Where is he staying? What has he been doing for the past seven years?

Her shoulders drooped as the full weight of the evening's emotions swept over her. Unbidden, a lifetime of tears rained down her face, and she wiped them away with the homespun skirt of Kathe's rough *cotte*.

A half hour later Edith's vigorous pounding on the heavy wood door finally roused Rosamund; she'd fallen asleep sitting on the floor in front of the fire with her head cradled on her arm that rested on the bench. And she'd dreamed . . . dreamed that she was walking with Erik in the garden at Burg Mosel and filling a basket with roses. Yellow roses.

* * *

Snow stung Erik's cheeks and clung to his eyelashes as he retraced his steps. The night sky was gray, and the rocks along the coast were gray, too. The earth and sky seemed to run together; it was hard to tell where one stopped and the other started when everything was shrouded in a misty veil of lightly falling snow.

Memories dominated Erik's thoughts. He pictured Lord Schmidden's daughter the way she'd been seven years ago: thin and gangly, with bright eyes that were too large for her small face. At the time, she'd reminded him of his younger sister, Karena, who was about Rosamund's same age, and her eager questions had made him feel important. He'd enjoyed telling her exciting tales from his seafaring adventures, and she'd listened in rapt wonder, often exclaiming, "Did you really?" and "Oh, how exciting!"

But little Rosamund had grown up.

He'd watched one friend after another grow soft toward a girl, but he saw now that their actions had only been the smoke of a volcano. Fire and darkness, ecstasy and terror, all rushed over him, and he was glad for the cold and the snow.

The more he thought about the last hour, the faster he walked. And the faster he walked, the more questions shot through his mind. Why was Rosamund living in that hut? And who was the gruff fellow who'd requested the mustard pot and delivered a veiled warning; he'd certainly been bold, quite as if he owned the place! And come to think of it, Rosamund had told him from the start that she was expecting someone else. Fear cast a long shadow over his heart. Was that churlish man her husband? He winced at the thought. Oh, surely not; she seemed so innocent. And yet . . .

Over and over, his mind replayed the evening's events. Over and over, he asked the same torturing questions. Questions without answers.

His steps slowed as he neared his crew's tents. Safely crossing the ice had filled him with exhilaration, but that experience seemed a lifetime ago. Now, all he could think about was the captivating Rosamund Schmidden.

# CHAPTER FIVE

Dark and brooding against the deep blue of the late January afternoon sky, Burg Mosel rose out of the white mist lying low in the surrounding valley as if floating on a magic carpet of clouds. A crimson winter sun spotlighted the stone residence's turrets and tower.

Inside his assigned room at the top of the keep, Erik stared at the orange and scarlet flames leaping in the fireplace and inhaled the fragrant scent of the burning pine sticks added to the fire for their color and aroma. The blaze threw lively patterns against the bare stone walls and created gloomy shadows that skulked behind the dark brown curtains enclosing the bed.

Erik surveyed the room while he waited for a servant to take him to meet with Lord Schmidden. A square wooden chest to the right of the duvet-covered bed held a pitcher and bowl. A towel hung on a nearby peg pounded into the wall. Sprawling in front of two straight-backed wood chairs, a brown bearskin rug with claws intact and muzzle resting on its chin warmed the floor. A low three-legged footstool rested in front of one of the chairs and a six-arm candle stand stood between them. The farthest corner held a large copper tub for bathing. It was definitely a man's room, sparse and utilitarian.

When Erik and his crew had arrived at Burg Mosel, capable servants quickly assigned the men to guest quarters in the west wing of the castle. All except Erik. A servant had led him through the main entrance and along a corridor that passed chained-shut double doors and ended in the curving stairwell of the castle's stone tower. On a clear day his top-of-the-tower room would undoubtedly have a commanding view of the valley and villages below, but today the heavy mist obscuring the surrounding lowland suited his melancholy mood.

The miracles of a willing crew and a frozen sea had filled him with faith and anticipation; however, his thoughts obsessively revisited a humble cottage on the coast. Each time he closed his eyes he saw Rosamund as he'd last seen her—shining waves of dark hair; rosy, dimpled cheeks; smiling lips; clear, violet-blue eyes—a feminine shape framed in an open doorway.

If it wasn't enough to think about her all the time, tormented by the thought that she might belong to that surly fellow who'd demanded the mustard pot, now he must stay in her home and converse with her father as if his personal world hadn't just been struck by lightning.

When he heard footsteps coming up the tower steps, he straightened his shoulders and deliberately made up his mind to accept whatever he learned about Rosamund's status as part of God's plan for him.

Rap. Tap. Tap.

Erik answered the knock on the door and followed the servant out into the stone stairwell and down the steps that deliberately wound to the left to give the defender in a swordfight the advantage. At the bottom of the stairs they turned and again passed the set of doors secured by chains. Erik jerked his head around for a second look. Noting the chalice and grapes carved on one door and the loaf of bread resting on a tray depicted on the other, he recalled

Rosamund's statement that her father had turned his back on God. Well, that explained the chains.

"What have I gotten myself into," he muttered under his breath as he hurried to keep up with his guide.

The corridor emptied into the vast central entrance hall, where pairs of dark eyes stared down at him from stiff, canvas faces hanging in frames on the walls. Shrugging off the feeling that he was being scrutinized, Erik followed the servant across the entrance hall and into the corridor that provided access to the dining room and great room.

Lord Schmidden was already on his feet when Erik entered the great room, and he hurried toward his guest, his warm hug and hearty greeting spanning the years since they'd last seen each other.

"The sight of you is a relief to my eyes, Branden. I can't tell you how grateful I am that you came."

In spite of Lord Schmidden's warm welcome, the twitching muscle in his left cheek betrayed an inner agitation. He drew a pair of over-sized chairs facing the roaring fire and motioned to Erik to be seated.

Turning to the carved-front sideboard, Lord Branden lifted a decanter and filled two pewter goblets with mead while Erik moved past a large pedestal table in the middle of the room that displayed the jade bust of a young woman on an ebony platform. His gaze took in the several cushioned settees and a collection of gilded chairs that lined the walls. Hanging from a long rod, a tapestry filled the wall above a long, narrow table that featured a pair of massive Chinese porcelain vases embellished in blue, orange, and gold.

As his eyes moved to the far side of the room, he looked through tall mullioned windows framed by heavy shutters and green velvet draperies. A box hedge surrounding a snow-covered garden of rose bushes filled the courtyard, and snow topped the marble bench resting in one corner.

Erik's gaze returned to the great room. A knight's suit of armor and a low, wooden stool rested near the fireplace, and their two chairs, large and sturdy and obviously chosen for comfort, each with arms and legs ending in curled paws and featuring a lion's head carved into the top rail's crest, stood waiting.

A tall man could stand inside the belly of the fireplace, and Erik guessed it was probably wide enough for five or six large men to line up side by side in its mouth. Its massive size suited the vast room and served as a base for the life-size canvas hanging over it.

At first glance, Erik caught a sharp breath; for a fleeting moment he thought Rosamund had come to haunt him. On second look, he realized it must be her mother, but the resemblance was remarkable, and he forced himself to look away for fear he would embarrass himself by staring.

As Lord Schmidden approached with their goblets, he said, "It's the fireplace I come here for. It's the best one in the place." He sighed and motioned his head toward the painting, "My wife's likeness has been in storage for years—but I got it out last week."

Momentarily taken aback by his host's reference to his wife's portrait, Erik merely nodded as he lowered himself into the empty chair by the fire.

From that point, conversation flowed easily between the two men. They drained their goblets and discussed Hansa squabbles and land management as they caught up on the past seven years. Despite Rosamund's comment about her father's angst at God, when Lord Schmidden mentioned his urgent request for assistance, Erik didn't hold back in describing the revelation that led to his crossing the sea on unprecedented ice, and he concluded by asking, "What is your current situation, my lord? How can I be of help to you?"

In a few short sentences, Lord Schmidden outlined the border raiding and his efforts to restore peace. "I foolishly thought things had settled down, but when we returned to Burg Mosel at the end of summer, Lord Frederick's estate manager, a black-eyed devil if I ever met one, paid me a visit. We sat talking, right here, just like you and I are doing. At the point when I thought we were ready to finalize the details of an agreement, he asked me about Rosamund—you remember my daughter?"

Erik's heart started to pound. His mouth went dry and his hands clenched on the chair arms. He could feel the heat rising up his neck, staining his face; knowing the truth about Rosamund's status could easily destroy his fragile hope.

Lord Schmidden stared into the fire, his bushy brows bowing so low they collided above his nose. And when he finally spoke, his words filled Erik with dismay. "He asked her age and if she was married.

And did I have other children? I reluctantly answered his questions. And then he told me Lord Frederick had met Rosamund that spring when she'd been out walking with a servant girl. He said his master was impressed by her beauty and spirit—and he wanted to marry her."

Erik broke out in a cold sweat and braced himself. He'd already decided not to ask questions about Rosamund; when he knew if she was free, then and only then would he be in a position to pursue her hand. And even if she *was* free, her father might not be willing to consider him as a suitor. Or she might not be interested in him.

But surely her eyes had given him hope.

Lord Schmidden leaned forward to confide, "I may not be a seer, but I know Lord Frederick doesn't care a boar's head about my girl. He's ambitious, that's all. Rosamund is young and beautiful now, but how could I be sure that once my property was safely in his pocket he'd still be kind to her, especially as she ages. Or to me, for that matter. I'd just be a stone under a pestle." He smacked the base of his empty goblet into the palm of his free hand to emphasize his point.

"So what did you tell him?" Erik unconsciously held his breath.

"I told him 'No,' of course."

"And that's why he threatened an all-out war?"

"Precisely."

"And . . . your daughter?" He found he couldn't say Rosamund's name. "How did she feel about all this?" He must know the whole truth.

Lord Schmidden stood up and reached for Erik's goblet. When Erik declined a refill, his host turned to answer, "I didn't tell Rosamund about Dagon's visit or Lord Frederick's marriage proposal," he shrugged, adding, "and I didn't tell her about asking you for help."

Erik could feel the perspiration slowly trickling down the side of his face but he couldn't make his arm move to wipe it away.

Lord Schmidden continued, "Earlier this week I sent her to stay with Edith, my childhood nurse. So even if I'm defeated, at least she'll be safe. And now that you're here, well, I'm confident that won't happen."

He banged the empty goblets down on the sideboard with a reverberating thud and stared pensively at his wife's picture. "I miss Rosamund fiercely—she looks just like her mother; that's why I hung my Rose's portrait back in its place. I had put it away after—well, I just couldn't bear to be reminded of what I'd lost."

Erik forced out his words, "With God's help I will not fail." He made it a vow. But the room felt suddenly too warm and sweat oozed from every pore in his body.

Scooting his chair away from the fire, Erik stretched out his long legs and leaned his head back. As he closed his eyes, the tension left his body. Rosamund was free. Gone was the fear that he was attracted to another man's wife. His heart bounded up to the ceiling.

Lord Schmidden returned to his chair and the two men sat on in companionable silence, watching the flames, each thinking his own thoughts.

When the fire died down, Lord Schmidden got up, stirred the embers, and then fed the fire. He poked at the logs with a fire iron and within a few minutes they snapped and spit and radiated heat. Standing with his back to the rekindled flames, his host began to talk. Erik got the impression that now that his problem had a solution, he could finally share his inmost thoughts.

"Aggressors continue to push to conquer the world. Just look at France and England; they've been at war for over fifty years. The desire for power seems to be part of the human condition. Whoever marries my daughter will gain control of the largest section of land in this region.

He turned and stabbed the blazing logs again. "And there's far more at stake here than my property and Rosamund's future." He leaned the iron poker against the fireplace and dropped heavily into his chair. "If I'm defeated, every lord around us will eventually lose his land, either by war or by surrendering to save lives."

Lord Schmidden brought a heavy boot up to rest on the knee of his other leg. "Years ago, the Romans came, bringing their government with them, and they confiscated the possessions of anyone who didn't support or conform to their system." He shrugged. "As I see it, some things never change."

Restless, he stood again and moved back to the fireplace. Grabbing the fire iron, he stabbed roughly at the flaming logs. Still clutching the tool, he swung around and stated aggressively, "This is Schmidden property." He pounded the iron on the hearthstone. "Has been for five generations. And I wouldn't take kindly to giving service to another."

Erik sat silent, thinking. When he finally spoke, it was with caution, "I've travelled the trade routes, and I know your concerns are justi—"

Loud voices in the entrance hall interrupted Erik, and the two men strained to hear the cause of the disturbance. Within moments, footsteps tapped along the corridor, and then a flustered maid appeared in the doorway. Dropping a quick curtsey, Matilda stammered out that Lord Frederick's estate manager was demanding to see Lord Schmidden.

"Show him in, Matilda," Lord Schmidden directed. He squared his shoulders and got to his feet.

Erik stood, in solidarity.

Within moments, Matilda reappeared, followed by Dagon, who strode past her toward the two men, tension emanating from his burly figure.

Before Lord Schmidden had a chance to extend a polite greeting, Dagon spoke aggressively. "Since my last visit, Lord Frederick has anticipated your consent to his proposal." His black eyes narrowed menacingly; there was no question that this was not a social call; each word held a veiled threat. "He offers the Lady Rosamund his deepest regards and expects me to arrange the ceremony as soon as possible."

Lord Schmidden's face flushed and his fingers clenched the back of his chair until the skin stretched taut over his knuckles. A low growl rumbled in his throat.

Erik broke in, his voice smooth yet carrying the weight of one who expects to be obeyed without question. "There is no message for Lord Frederick today." Erik took several steps toward the man. "Please allow me to show you out."

Dagon's eyes narrowed to dagger points. "We will expect to hear from you shortly." The words were polite enough, but the tone was demanding.

Erik escorted him out the door and along the corridor to ensure his departure.

Lord Schmidden had regained his composure by the time Erik returned, but he boldly voiced his astonishment, "Why didn't you tell that devil that never, under any circumstances, would I agree to give my Rosamund to Lord Frederick?"

"Well, my lord," Erik hesitated, taking care with

his words, "I'd say that discretion is the key to winning a war. A message sent through the enemy's agent will inevitably be altered by the time it's delivered.

Lord Schmidden nodded vigorously and heaved a relieved sigh. "Ah, yes, I can see your point. So where do we go from here?" It was obvious his confidence in Erik's judgment had raised another notch.

## CHAPTER SIX

A February blizzard tormented the sky and whipped the seacoast village of Altwarp for three long days. No one, not even the hardy Edith, dared to venture outside. Angry winds screamed at each other, and Edith's hut creaked and shuddered in the crossfire. Rosamund, unaccustomed to living in such close contact with the natural elements, not to mention Edith's nightly snoring, managed only fitful spurts of sleep.

Early in the morning on the first day of the storm, Edith had cautiously tried to open the door to survey the outside world and bring in more wood, but the ripping wind nearly tore it from her hands. She finally gave up and informed Rosamund they would need to carefully ration her meager stash of split logs stacked beside the fireplace if they hoped to stay warm for the duration of the storm. Then she slid the rough bench close to the hearth and steadied it with a chunk of bark wedged under the short leg in an effort to make herself and her guest as comfortable as possible.

Never idle, Edith pulled down stalks of dried mustard, comfrey, chamomile, and feverfew from the rafters, releasing their pungent tang and accumulated dust into the air that caused them both to sneeze. She explained to Rosamund that in order to be useful, the various herbs had to be collected at differing stages in their development. With a chuckle, she credited looking forward to gathering the next herb crop with keeping her alive these eighty-seven years. She went on to explain that garnering more herbs than she needed for her own purposes allowed her to barter at the annual village fair for goods provided by other villagers and itinerant fair merchants who followed the trade route and stopped at the small villages along the way.

Rosamund held a kettle in her lap and snapped free the brittle feverfew leaves from their stems, allowing them to drop into the pot. The discarded stems crackled merrily in the fire, while the mound of leaves in her kettle steadily grew under her nimble fingers.

Two weeks had passed since "The Night of the Book," as Rosamund called it in her thoughts. She hadn't spoken to Edith about her discovery or Erik's visit. Sensing that disclosing such a significant event to someone else might lessen its value, she'd hesitated, wanting to talk yet reluctant to spoil the wonder of her experience. However, her bright eyes brimmed with her unspoken thoughts. Once she even opened her mouth and then, pausing a moment, pressed her lips firmly closed. Several times her hands fell idle as she stared into the fire.

Rosamund's wistful thoughts finally broke into words. "Edith . . . ?" She faltered and then continued, "Will you tell me about my mama?" The precious word fell softly from her lips.

Looking up from the herb bundles mounded at her feet, Edith halted in her work. She rested her arthritic hands on the sides of her kettle and scrunched up her wrinkled face. "Why, *Liebling*, there's nothin' I'd rather be talkin' about."

She paused, as if sorting memories piece by piece. "English, she was. And, oh, so pretty." She craned her neck and her faded blue eyes looked through Rosamund as though she were seeing someone else. "Her picture ye be." She blinked and gave a little jerk that made her head bob. Her fingers resumed snapping herb leaves from their stems.

Rosamund watched her without speaking, wondering if she'd say any more.

After a lengthy period of silence without looking up, Edith continued in her own roundabout way. "Master Klaus—that be your papa—be meetin' her first, he did. On one of them there tradin' trips. Ja, ja. He went with my Lord Schmidden. His papa. 'Twould be your grandpapa, now wouldn't it?"

Obviously not expecting a reply from her young guest, Edith mused on. "Smitten, he was." She grinned an almost toothless grin and waggled her head. Frizzy silvered hair, what there was of it, only added to her wizened appearance. "Never have I seen a lad so besotted. Ach, quite offen his head, I tell ye."

She frowned and blinked rapidly, as if to focus her mind on details. "When plans be set for the weddin', Master Klaus flashed about like a courtin' grouse. And Burg Mosel saw the scrubbin' of all time. He said things must be jes' right for to be bringin' home a bride, but he couldn't be seein' straight for to do a blessed thing." She chuckled to herself. "And when your lady mother was come, well, then we be understandin'. We took to her in a blink, even me Lady Clara—and a hard one to be pleasin', she was. And I should know. Twenty years I be workin' for me lady."

Rosamund forgot the herbs. Her hands rested idly on either side of her kettle. With her bright eyes fixed on Edith, she absorbed every word.

The old woman rambled on. "Lady Rose loved to ride, she did. And your papa, he be buyin' her a mare. Black it be, and shiny in the sun. She brushed it 'til I 'spected its hair would be fallin' out for certain. Windy, she be callin' it. I heard tell your papa be up and sellin' her after your lady mother . . ." Edith's words faded with her breath. She stared into the fire, her lined face creasing into even deeper folds.

After a moment, her moist eyes narrowed intently as she switched her gaze to Rosamund. "Pfeffer, he's bein' Windy's colt. You be knowin' Pfeffer?" she questioned as if Pfeffer were a person.

Rosamund murmured an assent, but Edith's mind had already wandered aloud down another memory. "And the big singin' machine what Lady Rose be learnin' to play. And that Frenchman what be teachin' her; him's what be makin' eyes at me lady. I heard her tellin' him to be leavin' her alone—she what be lovin' Klaus an' all."

Stunned, Rosamund froze. But Edith, oblivious to the disconcerting effect of her disclosure, continued to bounce across her memories like a pebble skipped on a pond.

"So kind, your lady mother. Always doin' for others. When me Lord and Lady took the black sickness, she said we must be lettin' her nurse them, seein' as they was like her own folks. Like that, she was. And when they both died, it went so hard she couldn't save them that we be fearin' for her mind."

Edith rubbed her bleary eyes with a gnarled, arthritic hand and sniffed. "I thought belike she'd wear out a bench in the chapel, sittin' in there. Seems her need be somethin' we couldn't be givin' her." Again she fell silent.

Rosamund stared into the fire.

Edith sighed. "Your papa, dear boy, took to worryin' himself to a shadow. He set his mind to be sendin' her to the hot springs at Karlovy Vary, but she wouldn't be havin' any of it. Stubborn girl she be, your lady mother. But we sure be lovin' her."

When the glazed look in her eyes and another silence indicated that Edith's mind was off again on another tangent, Rosamund bit off her impatient questions. She'd waited years to learn about her mother, and she didn't want to ruin her opportunity by pushing too hard, but her desperate longing was all that made the long spaces between Edith's short bursts of conversation tolerable. Finally, she reached out and touched Edith's hand, whispering, "And then what happened?"

Edith turned to Rosamund, her eyes resuming their focus. "Why, 'twas the strangest thing ye ever did be tellin'. In one day she be her fair self again. Jes' like that. In fine fettle. We all be most catched by wonderment."

"Yes?" Rosamund barely breathed the word.

"She said, sure an' I'm sittin' here, that God spoke to her." She wrinkled her forehead until her brows—what was left of them—darted toward her nose. "I don't rightly mind how that could be. God never spoke to me, nor anybody's I be knowin'." She shook her head. "But belike 'twas a dream or a vapor. Naught of us be knowin'," she straightened her back and almost sang out the words, "but we was gladdened for certain to be havin' our dear Rose back."

Rosamund's eyes grew wide as her heart leaped in her chest. Rose, her own precious mother, had felt God's presence like she had.

Edith continued her reminiscing, unaware of Rosamund's joy. "Then you was on the way, and I know'd I'se bein' too old to be nursin' ye. That's when I be comin' here—where I growed up, you know."

Edith set aside her pot of herb leaves and shuffled over to the fireplace. She stirred the vegetable stew in the iron kettle hanging from an iron arm in the fireplace pit and then ladled generous portions into hard-bread trenchers.

After they finished their meal, Edith commented, "It's sure to be gettin' colder, Rose." She called her by her mother's name, as though they were one and the same. "The flames be comin' blue so it's to stop snowin', it is."

Groaning that sitting made her stiff, Edith got to her feet and limped to the door. Leaning into it, she slowly heaved it open. True to her prediction, the wind had died down and it had stopped snowing. Although she barely opened the door for a peek, snow cascaded inside from the drift deposited in the doorway like a homeless vagabond seeking shelter from the wind.

Edith whisked up the rapidly melting snow, but her mind seemed to still be on their earlier conversation, because she picked up where she'd left off before serving the stew. "Your lady mother loved the snow, she did. She'd go trampin' in it, be makin' trails with her little feet—she had little feet, you know—and then your papa, he'd be followin' her trails to find her. Laugh, they would, when he'd be findin' her. 'It was a game,' she said."

* * *

Rosamund continued to work the herbs, but often she would scoop up the leaves already heaped in her kettle and let them trickle slowly through her fingers. Like her thoughts.

Edith sagely observed this preoccupation, and waited. Her homely intuition proved right, and Rosamund voiced a second question. "Edith, did anyone ever, that is, were you ever particularly fond of someone? A man, I mean." Rosamund's dark lashes brushed her pink-stained cheeks and screened her eyes.

Edith wanted to laugh and cry at the same time. Laugh, because Rosamund was yet so delightfully sweet and innocent. Cry, because she remembered when Rosamund's father had asked her a similar question. Ensuing love had brought him supreme joy and intense anguish. And now his Rosamund teetered on the threshold of her future. The girl's face betrayed her heart, and Edith wondered if love would bring her happiness or sorrow.

She kept these thoughts to herself and instead answered Rosamund's hesitant question. "Ach, Dearie. Pleasin' to the eyes I be once. Ye'd never think it to be lookin' at me now." Her hunched shoulders quaked with her mirth. "Near ready for the hereafter I am." She pinched a prune-wrinkled cheek. "Me heavenly birthin' sack's over-ripe, so 'tis!"

Rosamund raised her dark brows and swallowed her amazement.

"There be two young men what set store by me, they did. I had to be choosin'. Richard Schwartz, him it was what be pesterin' the patience out o' me. He'd got himself the best prospects, he did, but he wouldn't be takin' kindly to hearin' 'No' for ought. He'd be gettin' angered easy and blamin' everybody less himself." She eyed Rosamund shrewdly. "I 'spected if I be choosin' him, he'd be angered at me the most 'cause I'd be in his door, comin' and goin'."

Rosamund listened with her mouth slightly open, as if drinking in words she thirsted to hear.

Edith's head bobbed several times to affirm her conclusion before she continued in a slow and dreamy manner, obviously reliving the throes of first love, "And then there be Alfie, Alfie Baer. Him it be what was sweet on me. His big brown eyes would be meltin' me heart jes' like that there snow, so's I could hardly be breathin'."

Edith's faded eyes lit up just thinking about Alfie. She drew up her shriveled body and lifted her ample chin. Preening, she caressed her cheek and ear with a gnarled, brown-spotted hand. As if she were still young and beautiful, she confided, "So I be choosin' Alfie."

After a pause, Edith continued her musing, "Richard said I'd be livin' in regrets. Later he be marryin' to Gertie Lund, she be havin' an eye for nice things. But I heard tell he'd beat her betimes. I be guessin' what there be things more 'portant in life than good prospects, and I never was regrettin' me choosin' Alfie. He didn't never get so fixed with earth's possessions, but his be a kind heart in his breast. So happy, we was. He wast be gone now for many a year, but my lovin' him jes' never dies. Him's what's still been livin' in me heart to this 'ere very day." Edith stared into the fire, forgetting her guest, alone with memories only she could see.

* * *

Rosamund sat motionless, unwilling to disturb the musing old woman, but her thoughts drifted from Edith's story to Erik. His blue eyes had certainly taken her breath away. And she knew from past experience that he was thoughtful and kind. But how was she to know if he was right for her? What if Edith had chosen Richard? And what about those who had no choice? She knew that was often the situation. What then?

The old woman gave a little bounce on the bench and her words interrupted Rosamund's thoughts. "Ach, I jes' be seein' the past, *Liebling.* Maybe you'st be seein the future?"

Startled by Edith's intuition, Rosamund sucked in a surprised little gasp, blushed, and looked away from the old woman's knowing gaze. As her eyes sought a resting place, they fell on the marriage chest that had belonged to her mother.

*Later,* she thought, *I'll get out the book and read a bit. Maybe God will speak to me again.* She glanced back at Edith and smiled shyly for her answer.

That evening, when steady, deep snoring confirmed Edith's sound sleep and held the promise of solitude, Rosamund slipped from the straw bed and knelt beside the waiting chest. Taking care not to make any noise, she opened the heavy lid. This time, without pausing, she quickly drew out the contents, intent on only one thing: the book. Holding it firmly in her grasp, she curled up on the floor beside the bench in front of the fire and tucked her stocking-covered feet under the skirt of her nightdress. She bit her lips between her teeth as she unlatched the clasp and opened the cover. Immediately, she retrieved the yellow rose and placed it on the bench.

She tipped the book so the firelight could shine on the page, and she read the curling Latin script:

*Hour One* began, "Blessed is the man . . ."

"I'm not a man," she impatiently mouthed the words and turned several pages before pausing at *Hour Four.*

*The Lord is my shepherd; I shall not want.*
*He maketh me to lie down in green pastures:*
*He leadeth me beside the still waters.*

As she read the psalmist's words she instantly sensed the uncanny Presence; a breathless warmth that reached to her toes. Galloping with Pfeffer had dulled her heart's lonely ache for a time, but this was different. That place of pain no longer hurt. It hadn't, she realized in surprise, since "The Night of the Book." It was as if fresh skin covered her old wound. Healing had blotted up her long-standing sorrow, and the haunting shadows of the past tormented no more. Yesterday and her mother both belonged to God. And she felt healthy. Whole. Safe in God's care.

*He leadeth me in the paths of righteousness . . .*

She verbalized her understanding of the words, "God will guide me."

She read another line, *I will fear no evil: for thou art with me.*

"Oh! God is with me—so I don't need to be afraid. And be with my papa, too, please," she tacked on her petition.

Through dewy eyes she made out the final words, *Surely goodness and mercy shall follow me all the days of my life: and I will dwell in the house of the Lord forever.*

She leaned her elbow on the bench and propped her chin in her hand as she mused over the meaning of the words. Yes, she understood: God's mysterious presence would always be with her—today, as well as in the future.

The temperature outside continued to drop, until eventually the chill in the room made her shiver. She slipped the yellow rose back inside the front of the book, refastened the heavy clasp, and hastily wrapped it in the silk scarf. She fitted it back into the chest and then replaced the other keepsakes. Gently, quietly, she eased down the heavy, hinged lid until she heard the spring click shut.

As Rosamund slipped back into bed and snuggled between the eiderdown comforters covering the straw, her thoughts returned to Edith's comment earlier in the day: *His eyes would be meltin' my heart, jes' like that there snow, so's I could hardly be breathin'.* Somehow, she couldn't help but think of Erik's blue eyes.

## CHAPTER SEVEN

Erik stood alone on the inner walking path near the top of the wide stone wall. He rested his elbows on the ledge of a tapering recess, one of many fenestrations built into the wall to protect sentries while providing visibility, and leaned into the crenel to view the whitewashed landscape. Frosted trees whiskered the distant rolling hills and curling tendrils of village smoke rose upward in clusters that dotted the countryside.

Erik's crew, sharpening their battle skills, engaged in archery practice in the stable yard. Erik could hear their shouts, like music to accompany his thoughts as he recalled his contact seven years ago with Lord Schmidden and Rosamund. Feste Burg, the Schmidden's military outpost on the coast, had represented his only tangible association with the nobleman and his daughter, but Burg Mosel's opulence gave him a new awareness of the Schmidden's cultural heritage.

Imported treasures of gold, silver, and porcelain filled the rooms, and Erik was amazed that a young woman like Rosamund, accustomed to such fineness, could be so at home in that poor cottage. Instead of casting a frown on the humble dwelling, her presence had glorified it.

Her sweet delight in finding God through the pages of her mother's book rose to the fore of his thoughts, and a familiar ache filled his heart, a yearning that never stayed silent for long. He let his mind envision his dreams as reality. Surely Rosamund embodied all the womanly virtues he'd idealized over the years: beauty, grace, a quick mind, gentle ways, and a spirit that was sensitive to God. Had anyone ever been so perfect?

He'd considered speaking to Lord Schmidden about his feelings, but after the tour of Burg Mosel and recalling his status as a guest—and a property-poor foreigner at that, he thought better of his foolish impulse. His neck grew hot just thinking about the rejection his impertinence would likely incur.

Certainly, Lord Schmidden would have already

made plans for his only child's future, and he felt quite confident they would not include him.

To force his thoughts in another direction, Erik began to walk. His gaze took in the snow-covered fields, the twisting, frozen river, and the winding pathway leading down into the valley from the grand stone structure. It all served to impress upon him the gulf between himself and Lord Schmidden's beloved daughter. To entertain the hope she could someday become his wife would mean allowing his heart to long for that for which he would never presume to ask.

Contrasting his lowly station to Rosamund's noble status made him turn away from the open sky and plunge determinedly into the dark tunnel of steps winding down to the courtyard below. He must discard his dreams—purge them from his heart even as a doctor would purge bad blood. To entertain the dream of what he could not have would only keep him from fulfilling his purpose here. He knew he would have to subjugate his thoughts once and for all if he truly meant to do his duty and depart with self-respect.

He groaned. Making noble decisions was

certainly easier than living them out—that required calling up his soul's deepest resources.

As he stepped into the sunshine at the bottom of the stairwell, Erik encountered Lord Schmidden, and the older man greeted him with obvious pleasure.

"There you are, Branden. Did Curtis show you around?"

"He did, my lord," Erik replied respectfully.

"I want to review our weapons with you." Lord Schmidden talked while they walked along the box hedge and crossed the gravel yard toward the small stone building Lord Schmidden had referred to as the armory. "I really don't know what we'll find. There's been no need to defend ourselves for nearly a hundred years, and I've had no interest in fighting, even for sport. Everything is probably quite antiquated. But we can acquire what is needed.

Lord Schmidden drew an iron key from his pouch and inserted it into the keyhole. It grated as it turned. Thrusting his shoulder against the old oak door caused it to bend before it gave way. Lord Schmidden pushed it open and stepped into the dim, musty room. Erik followed him, and they waited a moment while their eyes adjusted to the gloom.

A quick inventory revealed mismatched pieces of armor: a heap of leg guards piled against the back wall, several helmets with rusted visors hanging on wooden pegs, an odd assortment of deteriorating leather vests lying in the right front corner, a dozen or so maces scattered across the floor in a disorderly fashion, and a row of swords, sabers, and lances, two dozen at the most, hanging on one wall.

A closer review told Erik that only eight of the swords were sheathed in scabbards and the lot sorely needed honing. Their usefulness seemed dubious at best. Even in the dim light it was obvious that this abandoned armory held no cache of formidable weapons.

When the dinner bell clanged, Lord Schmidden ruefully pinched his lower lip at the timely interruption and commented with a wry smile, "Well, Branden, let's go eat. We'll talk about weapons later on a full stomach."

April, 1423. Altwarp, Pomerania

## CHAPTER EIGHT

Plump cottontail clouds lazed in the early morning spring sky. The snow was gone, and a carpet of wildflowers—lupine, sage, clover, sorrel, poppies—nodded their bright heads and shared whispered nuances of sweet aroma in the faint breeze. Gentle white caps rocked the blue sea and distant amethyst mountains lifted still-white peaks in worship. It looked like a perfect day for a fair.

Through the open door, prisms of sunlight shone through the open door and played hopscotch on the floor of Edith's cottage as the old woman bent over the sleeping girl. Dark hair curled around Rosamund's shoulders and one bare foot peeked out from under the feather-filled duvet.

"Come, come, *Liebling*." Edith gave her guest a wake-up call. "We must be a'hurryin'!"

Opening one eye, Rosamund stared up at Edith

as though her spirit were returning from a distant place. She rolled over and sat up, stretching slender arms above her head.

"Today is the day," she exclaimed; the first day of the fair had arrived at last.

She sprang up from the low bed, caught Edith's hands, and pulled her into a nimble quickstep—and the two of them whirled about in the warm sunshine. Rosamund's nightdress ballooned out like a church bell, while Edith's shapeless gown twisted tighter and tighter around her lumpy shape until her aged body betrayed her willing spirit and she tripped over her own feet. Rosamund caught her, and they clung to each other, laughing with abandon like two giddy schoolgirls.

"G'on wi' ye!" Edith tried to sound severe as she pushed unruly hair away from her face, but as their eyes met their laughter began again.

While she exchanged her nightdress for one of Kathe's well-worn *cottes*, Rosamund listened to Edith discuss the village fair. "We be workin' all the winter for this day. Seems each of all us older villagers needs be havin' somethin' to keep our hands agoin' so's we be livin' to see the spring. Tradin' our doin's is such a merriment. And there'll be merchants what be comin' on the trade route. Certain of them be comin' every year. Like ol' Robert, what be makin' shoes. And Limpin' George, what be sellin' knives, swords, and weapons-like; he ain't never missed a spring fair since what I be livin' here, and nigh on to twenty years that be."

Hurrying to accommodate Edith's impatience, Rosamund followed her out the door and along the hard-packed trail toward the Buress hut, where the family wagon sat waiting to cart them all to the large village farther up the coast, where the annual fair brought in merchants and villagers from the surrounding area.

"Good mornin' to ye, Frau Buress," Edith greeted her neighbor as she came out of her home. "A right beautiful day it be, ja?"

"Morning, morning. That it be," Radmilla Buress responded as she lifted her four young children into the wagon and then climbed in herself.

Edith whispered to Rosamund, "Looks like they be all feelin' quite well ag'in. Mind you, if she be makin' those young'ns to be wearin' undervests, they wouldna be gettin' the croup. Iffen ye be dressin' too light, ye be gettin' a chill." She shook her head disparagingly. "But there be some people what jes' won't be listenin', no how."

Edith's criticism made Rosamund eye the Buress family members as they squeezed into the wagon, and she hoped their commotion had kept them from overhearing her benefactor's pithy comment.

When everyone was settled, Emil clicked his tongue at the team of horses and they started off with a jerk. The ride took over an hour, and along the way, Rosamund's anxiety level escalated. Although Edith had frequently mentioned the upcoming fair, Rosamund hadn't realized until this morning when Edith hurried her to the Buress's cart that the fair was not held locally. She'd felt so safe for the past few months that it had never occurred to her until now that someone attending the fair might possibly recognize her? And especially considering that they would be spending the day in a large village on the established trade route.

In wagons and on foot, folks from out-lying villages filled the trail and streamed over the countryside, braced, armed, pulling, encumbered with all sorts of strange and unwieldy appendages including woven reed baskets and mats, home-dipped candles, hand-carved candlesticks and stands, homemade three- and four-legged stools, bleating goats leashed on ropes, and squawking fowl in homemade cages. Barnyard smells tweaked her nose and the din of activity could be seen and heard:. animals baaing and braying, poultry crowing and cackling, and even the voice of a recalcitrant pig squealed intermittently above the rest.

When the cart finally came to a halt on the edge of the square, Rosamund cast an apprehensive glance around as Radmilla Buress helped her children climb out of the cart. When it came her turn, Rosamund swallowed her fear and jumped down and then turned to help Edith to the ground.

The two women clutched the handles on either side of their large reed basket filled with herb pouches and followed Frau Buress and her children into the square. Edith called out greetings to folks she recognized from previous fairs, and Rosamund made an effort to smile and nod at those who included her in their friendly responses.

The broad square was the size of the entire village of Altwarp, and today it had become a teeming marketplace. Booths, each a board balanced on a pair of crude sawhorses that was shaded by a fabric canopy rigged over a simple frame, filled the square. Here and there, animals were tethered to spikes or posts, and locals and itinerant merchants did their best to display their wares: bolts of fabric, leather bags and pouches, tin cups and bowls, copper kettles, silver amulets, rings and earrings, sisal ropes, leather shoes, swords and daggers.

During the house-bound days of winter, Edith and Rosamund had torn a large length of linen cloth into many pieces, each about a handbreadth square. Mounding a fistful of garnered medicinal herbs in the center of each square, they'd created pouches by gathering up the four corners and securing them with short lengths of homemade rope. The pouches would provide Edith with bartering power.

Emil Buress joined a group of men who helped the out-of-town vendors construct their booths, and when they were ready, he directed Edith to an advantageous location near the fabric booth.

After Edith had spread a blue cloth over their board, she suggested that Rosamund arrange an appealing display of the little herb bags. Handing them to her, two at a time, Edith visited amiably with passersby.

Rosamund knew that several of the larger villages on Schmidden property held annual fairs, and she'd listened with keen interest when Kathe had told her snatches of the fun that occurred at such events. But Papa had dissuaded her when, on one occasion, she'd asked to accompany Hilde and Kathe. So today she had every pore open, absorbing the excitement with all five senses.

Indeed, the animal odors made her nose twitch and the heat, dirt, and noise were unlike anything she'd ever experienced, but her delight was so strong that her fear subsided and she hardly noticed the distasteful aspects. Her cheeks glowed with excitement and her eyes danced, trying to take in every detail.

Kathe's shabby *cotte* couldn't hide Rosamund's loveliness, and many a fair-goer turned for a second look at old Edith's pretty assistant. The moisture of youth had been wrung from Edith in the inevitable progression from mortality to eternity, and the two women, the young and the old working side by side, presented a vivid contrast.

When Edith was satisfied with their display, she gave Rosamund instructions on how to tend the booth alone while she visited the other vendors. "Be havin' a look-see," she said.

Nobody bartered much early on while it was still cool. People moved about from booth to booth, greeting each other, discussing the weather, the husband, the wife, the children, Aunt Millie, the lame cow, the tabby cat's new kittens. They laughed and joked, admired each other's wares, and enjoyed the day as if it were a holiday.

Many of the out-of-town merchants had set up their booths the night before, and they had no lack of business from early morning. People lined up at Ol' Robert's booth to purchase shoes. Waiting their turn, mamas and papas with a stair step of children at their heels stood in the warm sunshine.

Ol' Robert displayed shoe forms to fit feet from infant to adult sizes and he offered six trunks filled with assorted sizes in one style each for men and women, and another ten trunks overflowing with children's shoes.

Ol' Robert's wife, Helga, assisted each family in turn to find the best fit for every child, and when an appropriate size wasn't available, Ol' Robert set about making a pair. His twenty-year annual appearance had minimized the need for a local shoemaker, and between his visits, families traded their children's outgrown shoes among themselves.

Womenfolk clustered around the fabric booth, where the brightly colored fine linen and gleaming imported silks awakened an appreciation for beauty in some and stirred up dissatisfaction with their homespun in others.

And Limpin' George, another repeat itinerant vendor, was surrounded by men discussing the latest inventions in weaponry. His highly polished daggers, some with fancy crossguards or carved handles, were of highest quality, he assured his customers, pointing out the excellent handle-to-crossguard fit, the extra-long tang, and the finger-tightened pommels that unscrewed to reveal a small hollow where a lock of a lady's hair, a love note, or bit of verse could be concealed.

His swords, too, were each handmade, and he loudly decried the common mass-produced Falchion swords as poor quality imitations of a skilled craftsman's custom work. And his horse-bows and back quivers caused more than one young man to drool.

And next to Limpin' George's booth, a gypsy wagon filled the space—much to Edith's concern, which she boldly voiced to Rosamund while they were setting up their booth. "Seems there's always bein' at least one of them there gypsy wagons at the fair. Mind, you be stayin' away; I've heard tell they steal wanderin' young'ns."

Rosamund had shuddered. Could that be true? Recognizing her own ignorance of the world beyond her sheltered upbringing, she decided Edith must have good reasons for her prejudice and she made up her mind to stay away from the gypsy wagon.

Socialization, an important aspect of village life, intrigued Rosamund because she'd always lived an isolated existence. Shy at first and then more confidently, she participated in conversations with the visitors to their booth.

In the late morning, Edith returned and insisted that Rosamund take a turn visiting other vendors. Five-year-old Sarah, one of Radmilla and Emil Buress's daughters, had taken a liking to Rosamund and begged to accompany her, so the two set off together, a hot, chubby hand enclosed in a slender, cool one.

In the center of the square, continuous entertainment amused the fair patrons. An organ grinder and his monkey caught Sarah's attention, but she hid behind Rosamund when the monkey darted toward her. As Rosamund scooped her up and hurried away, three white dogs performing tricks on upside-down copper cauldrons made Sarah forget her panic.

They stopped to watch as the smallest dog jumped over the two larger dogs and landed safely. Sarah, secure in Rosamund's arms, clapped along with other spectators. But when the dog-master set fire to a hoop and swung it around, challenging the dogs to jump through it, Sarah started to cry and clung to Rosamund's neck, begging to go see the "ball-man."

An apologetic Rosamund wormed her way through the crowd. By the time they arrived in front of the jolly juggler demonstrating his tossing and catching skills, Sarah's tears had dried. When Rosamund stood her on her feet, her golden head bobbed, following the balls as they rotated rhythmically through one intricate routine after another.

The juggler's exhibition was followed by the performance of a painted-face mime who stood perfectly still while only his eyes rolled about in exaggerated movements. When he deliberately and elaborately winked at various ladies in the crowd, they blushed and looked away or clucked their tongues to disguise pleasure or express disgust. The mime winked at little Sarah, and she burst into delighted giggles. But when his eyes settled on Rosamund and remained there, staring, Rosamund immediately pulled a protesting Sarah through the crowd. A niggling sense of fear at being discovered continued to haunt her, and she promptly delivered Sarah to her mother and returned to Edith's booth.

When the sun shone directly overhead, many of the venders chose to sit near their booths to eat provisions brought with them from home. Others spread out blankets on a grassy knoll nearby.

Rosamund sank to the ground in relief as she and Edith joined the Buress family clustered on a blanket. Edith contributed a large loaf of rye bread and a bowl of shelled walnut meats to complete the meal of goat cheese and dried blackberries—berries that Sarah proudly announced she had picked "all by myself." They all washed everything down with gulps of homemade honey mead shared from a common family jug and listened to Sarah's animated chatter about the monkey, the dogs, the juggler, and the mime.

When the remains of lunch had been cleared away, Rosamund got to her feet. Edith had found a crate to sit on while tending her booth, so she suggested that Rosamund should take in the jousting match to be held in the early afternoon in a nearby field.

As Rosamund hesitantly set out, she got caught up in a cluster of people chattering excitedly about the various competitors, and her apprehension grew into anticipation.

When they reached the field and stopped behind a rope that marked the boundary on both sides of the jousting course, Rosamund looked around at the crowd beginning to gather. There were a few older couples standing close to each other, some holding hands, while the younger crowd teased and then giggled when a teenage boy tried to steal a kiss from a flirting maid. Rosamund smiled and turned her attention back to the jousting field.

Thoughts of Papa, of Erik, of Lord Frederick, were forgotten. Completely relaxed in her happiness, she observed the bustling activity taking place under the blue sky with its soft mounds of drifting white clouds. Had there ever been a more wonderful day?

In the next moment the clop of horse's hoofs drew everyone's attention. While everyone else shouted with excitement, Rosamund froze, rooted in dread. It couldn't be. Not on this bright, lilting day. She must be mistaken.

But she wasn't.

Astride a great black stallion at the jousting course's starting line, there was the devilishly handsome Lord Frederick, encased in a knight's armor, his dark hair gleaming in the sunshine. His stocky manager, Dagon, stood beside him on the ground, holding his master's helmet. The two men were the focus of attention and admiration. Surely this was her worst nightmare come to life!

Before she had time to react, Lord Frederick lifted his head, his dark eyes scanning the crowd intently. In the next moment, his gaze came to rest right where she was standing. With her heart beating in her throat, Rosamund ducked behind the tall blonde young woman standing next to her and then turned away, trying to wiggle her way through the people unnoticed, but fear that an arresting hand would grab her shoulder any second made her unsteady on her feet.

Crushed in tightly around her, the crowd kept her from falling but also prevented her making any headway in her effort to escape.

"You! Yes, you!"

Rosamund's whole being quaked; she'd never forget Lord Frederick's voice. Her mouth went dry and terror paralyzed her.

When no hand descended on her, slowly, reluctantly, she turned her head just enough to catch a glimpse of the blonde girl offering Lord Frederick her scarf, a token for him to wear in his bid for victory in the competition.

"And pray, tell me your name, Miss?" that haunting voice sent shivers down Rosamund's spine.

"M-Magda, my lord." The girl blushed and smiled coquettishly up at him.

With a bold wink, Lord Frederick wheeled his

mount and rode back to the starting line in an elegant display of horsemanship.

Tears of delayed shock and relief slid down Rosamund's face and her body started to shake, but the press of the crow held her tightly in place for the next two hours. Gradually, her curiosity superseded her fear; her tears and tremors eventually subsided and she found herself rooting for various contestants as the competition progressed amid shouts of elation over a champion's victory or insults hurled at defeated combatants.

However, to Rosamund's escalating dismay, Lord Frederick won match after match. The groundswell of public adulation focused on him as if he were a god, and when he was finally declared the tournament champion, concern for her father's conflict with Lord Frederick squeezed her heart in a vice of fear. This man was a formidable foe! Could her father really defeat him?

Rosamund wanted to rush back to the security of Edith and her herb booth, but the folks clustered around her were obviously the favored Magda's family and friends, and they weren't in a hurry to leave. Caught in the middle, Rosamund felt frantic to get away yet still terrified to make a scene that would draw attention to herself. Beads of perspiration broke out on her forehead and her body started to shake again.

"I'm going to be sick," she whispered to the people standing closest to her. When no one paid any attention to her, she said it louder and with more urgency, "I'm going to be sick—please, please let me pass!"

Like the Jordan River parting for the Israelites, the crowd parted enough to allow her to push her way through. But no sooner had she started along the pathway back to the village square than the tension of the day put her stomach in such a state of nervous upheaval that she ran over behind some bushes along the trail and fell to her knees as she vomited up her lunch.

When she finally sat back on her knees and raised her head, a quick glance toward the jousting field made her groan and collapse back into a prostrate position with her face to her knees.

*Oh no. Not again!*

Surrounded by admirers, Lord Frederick and Dagon were coming toward her on the path leading back to the square. Frantically praying to be invisible, Rosamund held her breath and waited for the crowd to pass.

Finally, when she could no longer hear their voices, she cautiously lifted her head and peeked around the bush that had protected her. Lord Frederick and his entourage had passed out of sight , but another cluster of returning fair-goers was coming her way. As soon as they had moved by, she leaped to her feet and unobtrusively attached herself to the rear of their group, hoping to blend in.

When they reached the village, Rosamund hurried through the busy square, intent on only one thing: returning to the safety of Edith's booth. As she approached the munitions booth, a group of about a dozen men stood gathered in front of it. Head down, she skirted them to get past.

"I've got a storeroom full of these."

Lord Frederick's familiar voice, cuttingly distinct, sent prickles of fear rippling over Rosamund's skin. Startled, her head came up and her eyes instinctively scanned the gathering for the owner of that voice.

And then she saw him!

At the center of the crowd.

Dagon stood next to him.

While she stared between villagers' shoulders in fearful fascination, Lord Frederick raised a long sword into the air, skillfully wielding it back and forth in smooth slashes. When the men standing closest instinctively jumped back, he let out a low chuckle and lowered the blade to rest in his free hand. Then in a shocking movement, he drew the honed edge over his thumb. Bright beads of ruby blood popped out along the slice, sending a foreboding chill down Rosamund's spine.

"And I'll be making good use of them soon enough," Lord Frederick boasted, sadistically rubbing his thumb along the blade and leaving behind a red smear. With another smooth movement, he raised the sword high and again flashed it about in sharp, whining slashes, its bloodied blade flashing in the sun's afternoon rays.

One of the gaping village men finally managed to put words to his shock, "Do you truly mean to attack someone?"

"I certainly do," Lord Frederick arrogantly lifted his chin as he carved the air with another hissing slash of the blood-stained sword, his bold, dark eyes moved slowly over the gathered crowd, feeding on their fear.

His smug smile gave way to a sinister sneer, "My neighbor is a constant source of irritation—but I doubt he can muster five hundred men to resist me."

Rosamund thought her heart would stop. He was talking about her papa!

Before her thoughts could progress, another peasant spoke up, "Why not settle your differences peaceably?"

This time Dagon growled a bitter retort, "He refused my lord's proposal of marriage to his daughter."

Rosamund felt the blood drain from her face. *Lord Frederick wanted to marry me!*

"Ho-ho! So . . . a war for a wife!" another villager exclaimed, interrupting her churning thoughts.

Lord Frederick shrugged; he obviously felt superior and safe in his derision.

"Is she a beauty?" a younger man called out, baiting him.

Lord Frederick waggled his eyebrows suggestively and his mocking grin smacked of blatant greed. "I want the man's property—but let's just say that marrying his daughter was not an entirely unpleasant prospect." His bold gaze slowly perused the men gathered around him and then returned to the one who had questioned him about her.

Rosamund's heart was pounding so hard she felt lightheaded. Clutching her arms around her middle, she gave herself ruthless orders. *You must not faint, Rosamund. If Lord Frederick gets his hands on you, Papa will pay any price to get you back, even if it ruins him.*

Hunching her shoulders, Rosamund turned to run away, but in her haste to escape she stumbled over the tether of a goat and landed on her knees. Panic-stricken, she kept her head down and slowly opened her eyes.

At the sight of a pair of costly leather shoes holding up a pair of well-developed hose-encased legs standing right in front of her, Rosamund suddenly couldn't breathe. Fear chased her mind down a path of terror: Expensive shoes . . . did they belong to Dagon? Had he seen her? Would he force her to marry Lord Frederick? And what would he demand of her poor Papa?

She slumped to the ground as everything went black.

* * *

Rosamund regained consciousness, but she didn't know where she was or what had happened to her. The first thing she noticed was the aroma—something sweetly pungent; unlike anything she'd ever smelled before. Barely opening her eyes to peek between her fluttering lashes, she abruptly sat up. Startled to find herself in an unfamiliar place, her gaze rapidly took in the little room as she tried to identify her whereabouts.

The feather bed under her completely filled the cubicle, and alternating panels in bright red and yellow covered the walls and draped the low ceiling of the space. A bright blue strip of fabric covered her lower body, but when she moved her hands and feet, she could see that she wasn't shackled or chained.

So how had she come to be here—wherever here was?

The din of animal noises and human voices just a bit too far away to distinguish words intruded on her solitude. She relaxed her fists that had unconsciously clenched the blue fabric draping her legs. At least she was not being carried off to Lord Frederick's castle on the back of his horse. Not yet, anyway!

She lifted her feet, first one and then the other, relieved to find that she was still wearing her shoes. Thrusting aside the blue fabric, she sat up and pushed her disheveled hair back from her widow's peak.

Then outside the room but quite nearby, a man's low, grating voice demanded intensely, "What do you want me to do with her?"

Rosamund froze in terror.

Another voice, more shrill and angry than the first, replied, "Sell her, you fool! Get rid of her!"

More frightened than she'd ever been in her life, Rosamund quickly scooted to the end of the bed and eased her body to a standing position, grateful to find that she was not dizzy or disoriented.

Hoping to discover a way of escape, she slipped between red and yellow curtain panels—and found herself face-to-face with a brown-skinned little old woman sitting quietly on a bench in the main area of what Rosamund instantly realized was a small, enclosed traveling cart.

The gypsy wagon!

When a toothless smile lit up the woman's face, Rosamund croaked, "H-How did I come to be here?"

Black eyes twinkled at her. "My son said you fainted, so he picked you up and carried you here. Did you take too much sun?"

Rosamund frowned and rubbed her eyes, trying to clear her thoughts. "Why—I don't know; I remember stumbling . . ." She caught her breath as the scene with Lord Frederick and Dagon flashed in front of her eyes. "H-How long have I been here?" She tried unsuccessfully to keep the panic out of her voice.

The old woman cackled softly. "You've been here a goodly while. But you are free to go if you feel all right." Thin, graying eyebrows arched over her beady eyes. "Maybe—are you in the family way, *Liebling*?"

As the woman's meaning became clear to her, Rosamund's face flushed scarlet. "No! No, I'm not married."

Eyeing her shrewdly, the old woman concluded, "Men fight over pretty girls."

Too near the truth for Rosamund's peace of mind, the sagacious comment sent her recklessly darting past the woman toward the front of the wagon. "Th-Thank your son for helping me. I-I have to go now." Before the men planning to sell her showed up to grab her!

As she cautiously poked her head out the front of the wagon between a pair of bright red curtains, she saw two men standing along the side of the wagon tugging at the goat between them. She let out her breath in a whoosh—they were quarreling about selling the goat, not her!

In the next second her eyes widened; the younger man was handsomely dressed and wearing the expensive leather shoes she'd seen just before her world went black. He must be the "son" who had carried her here.

Rosamund swallowed her relief. The old woman was right; she was obviously meant no harm and was free to go, so perhaps Edith's prejudices were unfounded after all.

With her head down, Rosamund scuttled away, trying to blend in with other fair-goers as she made her way back to the security of Edith's herb booth.

But even though she was safe, Rosamund's mind refused to rest; her distraught emotions tumbled violently over her rocky thoughts as she rehearsed the conversation between Lord Frederick, Dagon, and the village men. Instead of feeling flattered over Lord Frederick's offer of marriage as she once would have, Rosamund shook with anger and disgust at even being found attractive by such a vicious man.

And she wasn't quite sure whether it made matters better or worse, but to know that Lord Frederick didn't really want her—that she just provided a convenient means for him to get his hands on Papa's property—stung with the betrayal of a Judas kiss. Her naiveté had found Lord Frederick handsome and fascinating. Oh, the shame.

And now Papa's bewildering distress of last fall made sense, and she understood why he'd been so set on sending her to stay with Edith. Her insides seethed with white-water anger, and several times her indignation boiled up until she had to clench one hand in the other to keep her body from shaking.

In spite of Rosamund's fear that Lord Frederick and his manager would pass by Edith's booth, they never came. But she couldn't find the words to confide in Edith; it was almost as if telling what had happened would make it real.

When the booths were dismantled and she

climbed into the Burris wagon for the ride home, Rosamund hoped she'd finally be able to relax. But their basket was now awkwardly filled with two smoked hams, a length of hand-woven cloth, and a few left-over herb bags. Edith was tired, so Rosamund ended up balancing their basket on her lap.

Upon arriving at the Buress's home, Edith clambered to the ground and headed toward her own hut as if her feet knew every stick and stone even in the darkness. Rosamund was the last one to climb out of the wagon, and she trudged along behind Edith, carrying the basket that Edith seemed to have forgotten. After everything she'd been through that day, she jumped at every shadow and noise as she tried to see in the dark.

Inside the hut at last, Rosamund sighed in relief and turned to lower the crossbar. When she turned back into the room, Edith had untied the laces on her *cotte* and dropped it and her underdress on the floor as she crossed the room. Rosamund leaned against the door and watched her pluck her nightgown off the peg where she'd hung it that morning and tug it over her head as she reached the bed. Edith laid down, turned her face to the wall, and immediately fell into an exhausted, snoring sleep.

Lonely, homesick, and wishing she had someone to talk to now that she finally felt safe, Rosamund's eyes welled up with tears as she changed into her nightgown. The room was cold, and she shivered as she knelt by the fireplace. Prodding with the iron tongs, she stirred the cold embers until a tiny flicker and a small wisp of smoke indicated a spark of life. She breathed gently on it until the log she placed beside the spark actually caught fire, then she sank back and wiped her hand over her damp eyes. After adding two more pieces of wood to the fire, she scooted into the bed beside Edith.

But in spite of the long day, she lay in the dark listening to Edith's snoring while tears trickled out of the corners of her eyes. With every beat of her heart, her pulse pounded in her temples. And like stinging nettles, the nerves in her arms and legs tingled, causing her limbs to twitch. Determined not to disturb Edith, she lay there in torment.

Then it came to her. The book!

She sat up, wiped her eyes on the sleeve of her nightgown, and slipped from the bed, Fumbling in the fire's erratic shadows, she collected the candle in its holder and touched the wick to the burning logs until it ignited. Carefully shading the fresh flame, she crossed the room and placed the candlestick on the floor between the her mother's wedding chest and the bed.

With her lower lip pinched between her teeth, Rosamund frowned, concentrating on opening the clasp and removing the contents of the chest. When at last she again held the book in her anxious fingers, she impulsively hugged it to her chest.

In the next instant, she gasped. *How amazing that just holding the book brings comfort!*

Even though it had been generously warm during the day, in spite of the fire, Edith's cottage felt chilly. Rosamund shivered and inched back under the comforter. Propping herself up on one elbow, she lifted the ivory cover and carefully placed the yellow rose on the floor beside the candlestick.

She tried to turn the pages, but the awkwardness of the bed compounded by her trembling fingers made her lose her grip. The book scrolled shut as it slid off the feather ticking that served as a mattress. With a smothered exclamation of dismay and a quick grab, Rosamund caught it before it tumbled into the burning candle. She jerked it back onto the low bed and instinctively cast a nervous glance at Edith to confirm that she was still sleeping.

Taking deep breaths to ease her tension, Rosamund returned her attention to the book. Because the cover creaked as she lifted it, she quickly flipped the pages. It fell open to *Hour Four*. *I read that last time,* she thought, and quickly turned to the next page, *Hour Five*. Her gaze fell on words that seemed meant for her:

> *The Lord is my light and my salvation;*
> *Whom shall I fear?*
> *The Lord is the strength of my life;*
> *Of whom shall I be afraid?*

Rosamund whispered softly to herself, her thoughts filled with wonder, "The Lord is the strength of my life; of whom shall I be afraid?" She repeated it, "The Lord is the strength of my life; of whom shall I be afraid?" And again, "The Lord is the strength of my life . . ."

The shaking stopped. The throbbing eased. Her

nerves calmed. What was it about the words in this book that relieved her fears and brought peace and comfort?

She closed her eyes for a moment, wondering if the anxiety would return—but it didn't. Instead, a sense of quietness and peace filled her heart and mind.

She made herself recall Lord Frederick and his boasting and threats, but even those recollections did not revive the terror that had filled her spirit only moments ago.

Slowly releasing her breath in a relieved sigh Rosamund slipped the yellow rose back inside the cover and gently closed the book. When she'd laid it on the floor next to the candle, she extinguished the flame in one short puff.

With the comforter pulled up to her chin, she closed her eyes and murmured over and over, "Of whom shall I be afraid?"

* * *

Rosamund awoke the next morning to discover Edith sitting on the wooden threshold of the open cottage door. Her back rested against one side of the door jamb and her knees were bent. One on top of the other, her bare feet rested along the bottom end of the opposite doorpost.

Rosamund opened her lips to call out "good morning," but then she saw her mother's book, open and resting on Edith's lap. Dismay followed Rosamund's surprise. And then a rush of compassion filled her heart.

"Do you know what you're reading?" she gently questioned Edith.

Edith didn't apologize for having Rosamund's book. Instead, she closed the book and lifted sad eyes, her despairing words echoing in the cottage. "I canna be readin' it. No one ever be learnin' me."

"The book tells about God," Rosamund explained softly. "I can read it to you if you'd like." She sprang up from the bed and quickly moved across the room.

Dropping to the floor, she settled beside the old woman. Eagerly, Edith passed the book to her. When she'd opened it and turned to the presentation page, she read aloud her father's inscription. As Edith wiped at the moisture glazing her eyes, Rosamund turned to the back of the book and read the scribe's prayer.

*Lord, send the blessing of Thy Holy Spirit upon this book, that it may mercifully enlighten our hearts . . .*

"Oh, my, but it's bein' so beautiful," Edith exclaimed.

Turning to *Hour Twelve*, Rosamund read the words which had first touched her own heart. *"Oh God, thou art my God; early will I seek thee . . ."*

Edith listened intently as Rosamund continued to read: *"Because thy lovingkindess is better than life, my lips shall praise thee."*

Rosamund lifted her head, pausing to ask, "Do you understand that God loves you?"

The old woman's face creased into a million smile wrinkles and joy lighted her faded eyes as she nodded. "And I love him, *Liebling*; I do, I do!"

Rosamund responded to Edith's infectious delight with an exuberant hug. And during the remainder of the day first one and then the other would stop to say, "Let's read some more from the book."

## CHAPTER NINE

Over the long winter months, Erik had organized his crew into a training team whose primary goal was to sharpen the fighting skills of the village men in anticipation of a spring confrontation with Lord Frederick. To accommodate the training, the great room at Burg Mosel had undergone a major transformation. The elegant tapestries and costly furnishings were stored in the adjoining music room, hidden behind the heavy draperies that formed a partition between the two rooms. The whine and crash of clashing blades drowned all other sounds, and even though the windows stood open, the room reeked of unwashed bodies.

Erik looked up from watching Olaf engage in "parry, feint, lunge, and thrust" with a local farmer when Lord Schmidden stopped in the great room doorway. One of those men whose presence could be felt before he was seen, Lord Schmidden had been born to wealth and authority, and the respect shown him by his loyal subjects was well deserved; he'd been a kindly overseer yet a firm judge in matters of dispute.

Lord Schmidden's keen blue eyes under bushy brows searched the room until he located Erik. When their eyes met, he beckoned with a nod of his head and waited while the young man wove his way through the men and joined him.

"How's it going, Branden?"

"Very well, my lord." Erik spoke loudly to be heard above the din of swords, groans, and the occasional expletive.

The men were grouped in pairs, thrusting and parrying with vigorous lunges, and especially so with Lord Schmidden in their midst.

"Step out here with me." Lord Schmidden placed his hand on Erik's shoulder as they moved side-by-side through the doorway. Although about the same height, Erik's well-built frame in no way diminished Lord Schmidden's powerful build.

Halting in the corridor, Lord Schmidden turned to Erik. "Give me an update on the status of the men you've trained, the equipment and supplies, and your strategy for war."

With a gesture of his head toward the room they'd just left, Erik responded, "The men you saw in there are the final division. We've trained about fifteen hundred men from fourteen villages. They've been divided into units of archers, swordsmen, lancers on horseback, and those who will operate the catapult, cannons, and battering ram. All the supplies, equipment and horses have been procured and assigned. Members of my crew will lead each unit. I'll ride in front with the standard and signal directions."

Erik lowered his voice and turned his back to the doorway; it was his turn to ask questions. "Have you any news of Lord Frederick? Only three days remain until his deadline."

Lord Schmidden lowered his voice to match. "One of our scouts observed Lord Frederick mustering his men, along with those of two neighboring landowners. But he said they have no more than a thousand foot soldiers, so *we* have a numbers advantage. It seems he's unaware of our preparations." He grinned. "Won't he be in for a nest-ruffling?"

He continued, more soberly, "But we must move immediately if we expect our plan to strike first to succeed." He clapped Erik on the back and ended curtly, "Take it from here, Branden, and keep me informed." Turning on his heel, he strode down the corridor, his abruptness betraying his anxiety.

Erik returned to the great room and stood quietly for a moment, observing the engagements of the men and his crew. The strength and confidence demonstrated in their interactions sent hope soaring in his soul and reinforced his goal to take the battle to the enemy. Grabbing up the bell he used to indicate he wished to make an announcement, he rang it vigorously.

When he had everyone's attention, he said, "We'll be forming ranks tonight in the lower field. You are dismissed now to eat and get some rest. I'll see you at sundown. Karl and Olaf, I need to speak to you privately."

Erik dispatched the two men to ride through the countryside with a rallying cry for the village men who'd returned to their homes to await a summons after completing training exercises.

* * *

Waking with the first light of dawn, Erik lay on the hard earth, silently reflecting on the past day and a half. The men had assembled in the field two nights ago, and after assigning them according to their divisions to various sites for sleeping, he'd cautioned everyone to take the opportunity to rest, knowing the night would not be without difficulty. Fear and excitement would do their best to keep the men awake, him included.

Yesterday's march had proceeded according to plan. They'd followed the river, staying on the right bank. Moving nearly fifteen hundred men plus weapons and supplies proved a massive operation, and Erik felt grateful for adequate time to maneuver into a position that would give them the advantage. He recalled his surprise that they'd encountered no scouts or activity when they'd crossed over into enemy territory. Of course, Lord Frederick's land that extended up and out from the river *was* densely forested, and if he were to rally troops, they'd likely come from villages farther south and east. Still, Erik felt wary; it seemed too quiet.

He'd slept fitfully last night because he was worried. Not as another in his place might be, for he had no doubts about his mission or his strategy, but he felt deep concern for the men under his command and the families each represented. He closed his eyes and repeated the Lord's Prayer, requesting divine assistance:

*Our Father*
*Which art in heaven,*
*Hallowed be thy name.*
*Thy kingdom come.*
*Thy will be done in earth,*
*As it is in heaven . . .*

As he ended, Erik added his own request, "And Lord, today especially, I humbly beseech You to give us strength and wisdom. Amen."

With his heart at peace, Erik rose and gave the order to move out while it was still early and cool. Steamy morning fog rising from the river hovered in a thick silence that blanketed the surrounding lowland. It muffled sound and provided the men with a measure of cover. Erik took it as a sign that God was with them.

Each unit waited in readiness while their leader rode review. Those on horseback, one hundred twenty strong, took the position of vanguard. Dressed in full white armor: breastplates, shields, arm-plates, leg-plates and plumed, polished steel helmets, the mounted unit sat proudly on swift and strong rouncies and coursers. Bright banners of blue and white, carried high, gave courage to the rest of the company. Immediately behind them came archers in link mail and headgear, their bows in hand and the fletching feathers on the ends of their arrows sticking out of the quivers slung over their backs.

Next came *handgonners* carrying straight wooden stocks and eight-inch iron tubes to be ignited by poking a hot wire into the touch hole to set off the gunpowder. They were followed by foot soldiers wielding swords and maces. The men assigned to the food and baggage train brought up the rear.

Astride a majestic white destrier, Erik took his place at the front of the procession, his blue and white banner fanning out behind him as he rode. A commanding figure, he inspired the respect and devotion of those he led.

He turned his head to look back on the impressive entourage under his direction. A terrible silence choked the air and mute expectancy ruled every face. The thrill of a challenge —something he'd not felt in a long time—shot through Erik's veins. Indeed, he sensed that they pursued a holy mission.

Turning to Father Andrew, the local parish priest who'd joined them before they moved into Lord Frederick's territory, Erik invited him to pronounce a blessing on their endeavor.

In his deep voice, Father Andrew boomed out, "Almighty and eternal God, those who take refuge in you will be glad and will forever shout for joy. Protect these soldiers as they discharge their duties. Guard them with the shield of your strength and keep them safe from evil and harm. May the power of your love enable them to return home in safety, that with all who love them they may ever praise you for your loving care. We ask this through Christ our Lord. Amen."

Slowly, deliberately, they began the march to cover the final distance.

Because surprise was the key element in Erik's strategy, when they sited Lord Frederick's recently finished fortress on the outcropping in the distance, Erik grabbed the blue and white banner's wooden staff and lifted it out of its casing. Holding it high, he waved it vigorously in a silent signal to deploy.

A swarm of men set to work preparing the battering ram; it was a large tree trunk capped with a metal point and suspended on pulleys from the roof beam of a wood-slatted shed. A team of men covered the shed roof with wet hides to protect the ram and its operators from avalanches of enemy fire and hot tar, while others tightened the ropes that ran the pulleys and winches.

Another contingent rolled the catapult into an advantageous position on a knoll. It took several men to slide the lever into the appropriate groove so they could angle the stones for maximum loft. Others braced the wheels. Two men unhooked the twisted rope that provided the catapult arm's power, and ten men loaded its crotch with a large stone from the wooden cart stationed beside the catapult.

A third group of men rolled the two cannons into place while the handgonners set up their stocks.

Erik kept a keen watch on the remaining units as they maneuvered into predetermined positions. When everyone was settled in their places, he again raised the blue and white banner, the established signal to attack.

Ripping through the stillness, the shuddering

thunder of the cannons shook the earth as they spewed out flames and smoke. Towers and walls disappeared in banks of billowing smoke that hung motionless in the dead air. The die was cast.

When Erik spurred his horse to a gallop, the men on horseback followed his lead. Archers swarmed the hill. Bows twanged. Arrows whistled. Excitement surged to fever pitch. A forest of lances and banners approached toward the drawbridge. Foot soldiers grunted and groaned as they worked together to maneuver the catapult.

When there was no immediate response to this aggressive attack, a dreadful thought clutched Erik's mind: *Could Lord Frederick possibly have set out for Burg Mosel by another route?*

But no—sentries began returning fire from the walls, their projectiles whizzing through the air, knocking up the dirt where they struck. The drawbridge lowered and Lord Frederick's men streamed through the gate, armed and armored, straight into battle with a waiting confrontation of lances and arrows.

When the swarm of Lord Frederick's foot soldiers had crossed the drawbridge, it was immediately raised, preventing Erik's men from entering the fortress.

Erik's seasoned crew had trained the village men well, and each unit followed its leader. Erik observed the exchange of fire with satisfaction. But when the leader of the left wing of foot soldiers fell, wounded, Erik immediately handed his flag to his page and ordered him to keep it flying. Then he rode over and rallied the men. "Follow me," he commanded, beckoning them with his free hand.

And they did. All four hundred of them.

He led them eastward up the slope of the hill toward the fortress, where fierce and bloody battling ensued. Shouts, groans, and curses filled the air and added to the confusion. Man against man, hand-to-hand, with swords, maces, lances, arrows. Horses were felled, their screams intensifying the drama. Wounded men gritted their teeth and went on fighting if they were able; it was better to be half dead and standing than to be trampled to death underfoot.

The artillery attack continued, hammering away with all its might. The sun peaked and then began its descent. Lower and lower it sank in the sky as the long hours passed in a violent battle marked by streaming bright flags, explosions of red fire, and gushing plumes of white smoke—all stark against the gray sky.

Blood, sweat, and dirt mingled on each face. Cries and howls rent the air. Foot soldiers fought like a raging tide of destruction. Spears and swords flashed with the gleam of the setting sun.

Accompanying the turmoil, the archers' deafening yells rose as each sent his fiery messengers flying up, up, up and over the wall. The banners carried by the horsemen were countless, Lord Schmidden's sea of blue-and-white clashing with Lord Frederick's waves of black-and-red.

When at last, out of the near-darkness, a shout rang out from the wall above, bearers of the black-and-red retreated. And the blue-and-white went right along with them. Hacking. Lunging. Stabbing. Over mangled bodies, foot by foot, Erik's men pushed Lord Schmidden's enemies back into the fortress.

"Take over for me," Erik instructed Olaf before he quickly withdrew and returned to his page. The time had come for regrouping, and he gave the order for his page to sound the trumpet. Within minutes, his soldiers had redirected their attention to the wounded.

Bearers of the blue-and-white were carried down the slope and laid out in rows, to be tended as quickly and mercifully as possible. Because their groans and cries and the smell of fresh blood attracted vultures seeking carrion for an easy meal, he assigned a crew of men under the direction of Leif as guardians of the injured.

Dead bodies were carried farther down the slope and placed side by side, and a group of foot soldiers were set to digging graves. Father Andrew passed between the wounded and dying, praying for the injured and offering last rites; no one would suffer the indignity of a night without burial.

Lord Frederick's dead remained where they'd fallen, and the shadowy hillside was strewn with wasted bodies. It was a sickening sight. The blood. The mutilations. The dead faces. Blank eyes staring out in wretched ghastliness.

Darkness overtook them as Karl finished the final count of Erik's fallen: twenty-four dead, eighty-seven wounded, eight missing. Four hundred sixty-two of Lord Frederick's fallen men were even yet lying on the slopes around the fortress, representing a significant loss for the black-and-red.

Those not involved in caring for the wounded or burying the dead were separated into units and deployed around the fortress. Food and sleep were now paramount because sunrise would bring another bloody day. After each division had posted a watch, everyone sought rest.

Erik awoke before dawn. Immediately, his thoughts took a philosophical turn as he reflected on the previous day's battle. It seemed to him that in every war both sides are convinced that God is on their side—but the victory is decided, not according to right or wrong, but to bring about the purposes of divine will.

*So,* Erik mused, *what is my responsibility in this?*

Then quietly, into his spirit, came the answer. *It is for you to follow your conscience. If you do what you know to be right, you can trust God to work His purpose through the outcome.*

Inhaling deeply, Erik whispered, "Lord, I am Your servant; this battle is Yours."

At first light, Erik dispatched runners to the various divisions to inform them of the day's strategy.

And when each unit had confirmed its readiness, he raised the banner, signaling the attack of foot soldiers and horsemen.

Before the gate opened to allow Lord Frederick's foot soldiers to emerge onto the bridge, several of Erik's men braved the foul moat and scrambled up from below. Unseen by the enemy, they slashed through the heavy ropes that raised the drawbridge, thus opening the way for a frontal attack, with the main gate as the target, and eliminating the possibility of shutting out Erik's men.

The drawbridge dropped with a loud crash and the battering ram rolled across to begin its bludgeoning business. The beam lunged forward and then rebounded to re-engage and lunge again. Forward and back. Forward and back. Pounding away with all the strength of thirty-six sweating, work-hardened men.

Within minutes the fortress walkways teemed with enemy soldiers who dumped bucketfuls of stones down on Erik's men below. Others poured burning debris out through the machicolations. Posted guards called out warnings so the men could retreat in time to avoid injury, while archers picked off Lord Frederick's soldiers whenever they showed themselves.

Astride his horse, Erik sent up a second signal that moved the catapult and cannons into action. When the first shot of the catapult did very little damage, the men hastily reloaded. The wall, shaken in yesterday's assault, succumbed to the second shot. The mortar between the stones cracked. As Erik watched, an upper segment of the wall shuddered and then toppled into the moat. At the jubilant cry of the men manning the catapult, Erik's men fought with renewed vigor.

Meanwhile, the battering ram pounded repeatedly on the reinforced doors as the process of assault continued. Swing back. Re-engage. Propel. Impact!

Assessing the various elements of the offensive, Erik noted that the men operating the ram showed signs of exhaustion. Making a swift decision, he nodded at the trumpeter, and the horn's three short blasts sent a second crew leaping forward to replace the weary men.

At long last the heavy doors shuddered and groaned. Iron bracings ripped loose with the screech of metal tearing away from wood. A deafening roar of elation arose from Erik's men; breaching the entrance was a major step toward victory.

When the doors gave way, the men operating the battering ram quickly backed it out of the way to make room for foot soldiers. At Erik's signal the men operating the catapult arm re-engaged, tightening the sinew rope around the winch, securing the hook that worked the claw, and lifting a stone into place.

The first shot tore a hole in the bridge, cutting off traffic between the fortress and the surrounding countryside. Minutes later, the second strike launched a fifty-pound stone that smashed into Dagon on his horse as he thundered under the crossbeam of the main gate. Body parts went flying and his horse crashed into the moat, its agonized screams adding to the ear-splitting din.

Seeing that the stage was now set for a last furious struggle, Erik leaped to the ground, unsheathed his heavy sword, and joined a contingent of foot soldiers in their press into the fortress. Slipping and sliding over the dead beneath their feet, the blue-and-white drove back the despairing forces of the black-and-red, cutting them down by the score.

In the middle of the castle yard, surrounded by sword and pole axe-wielding soldiers, Erik came face-to-face with a taller-than-average soldier outfitted in a highly polished coat of mail that he instantly recognized as the work of a master craftsman. Peering through visor slits, their eyes met, the burning blue ones challenging the dark-eyed opponent. Without hesitation, Erik raised his right arm into the upper quadrant.

"Beware, my lord!" The warning cry of a nearby enemy soldier told Erik he'd met his nemesis.

He struck the first blow, recalling in that moment his father's pithy advice when as a boy he'd practiced his fighting moves with a wooden sword: *If you expect to win the fight, you must deliver the first strike. Before your opponent has a chance to retaliate, strike again—hard—for he who defends is always in danger.*

Erik followed his first strike with a sharp thrust aimed at Lord Frederick's throat.

His agile opponent jumped back, cursing viciously as he raised his shield. Then in a smooth arc, he raised his fine, narrow sword and sliced at Erik from the left side.

But Erik was ready for him; with a wide leap he thrust and jerked his blade up sharply.

But again, Lord Frederick pulled up and back, avoiding a clash, and then darted in to take another swipe at him.

This time Erik's blade connected with the flat side of Lord Frederick's sword and he lunged forward with his entire weight behind it.

But his skillful opponent's short, nimble side steps diverted the power of Erik's plunge and sent his heavy, hissing blade full circle through the empty air. It struck the stone floor with a resounding clang, jarring his neck and shoulders. His teeth chattered and stars flashed across his eyes.

"There's more where that came from!" Lord Frederick sneered, coming at him full force.

Erik sucked in a sharp breath, tightened his grip, and re-engaged in the fight. "In the name of God and Lord Schmidden, I shall defeat you!"

Leaping over a basket of stones, Erik chopped at his opponent, who dodged behind a wooden keg. His sword blade hacked a hole in the keg and sent a potent-smelling barley beer gushing over the stones. Slipping and sliding, panting and grunting, the two commanders battled their way back and forth across the courtyard.

Their swords whined. Metal armor clanked and chimed. Intent on thrusting and slashing, they ignored the clamor around them.

Upper body strength from working the ropes on The Tarragon's sails gave Erik the advantage of power, and he drove his opponent hard. And when Lord Frederick backed through an arched doorway, Erik plunged after him.

Instantly, his eyes burned at the mordant smell of smoked meat that slapped him in the face, but his helmet prevented him from wiping away the welling moisture. Blinking hard to focus, Erik gaped at the maze of skinned animals suspended on ropes from the cross beams; dozens of smoked carcasses filled the room, blocking his vision.

"You're not from this province, are you? I should have guessed Lord Schmidden would have to hire himself a commander . . . so what's in this for you? The girl?" The angry taunt came from behind a swaying stag that set off a cloud of flies. "Did her daddy promise you a pristine maiden?"

Erik growled low in his throat.

His opponent's jeer swelled with triumph. "That's it, isn't it?"

Incensed, Erik lunged toward the voice. Swinging his head back and forth to ward off the flies, he hacked and sliced off chunks of the trussed up carcasses with his sword as he charged forward. Joints, ribs, animal heads thudded to the floor as he charged toward the stag.

"Trust me, she's a tasty little morsel," Lord Frederick gloated. "She came to me—last spring."

His devilish chuckle made Erik's blood boil; in one powerful swing, he cleaved the stag in half from top to bottom, the tip of his sword screeching as it caught Lord Frederick's breastplate behind the carcass and split it wide open at the same time.

Leaping back with a vile curse, Lord Frederick took refuge behind the nearby carcass of a wild boar. Clutching at his breastplate, he used his shoulder to shove the stiff pig toward Erik's advancing figure as he sneered, "Did her father tell you *that*?"

Erik dodged the oncoming carcass and caught fleeting glimpses of silver armor between swaying pendulums  as his opponent deliberately heaved them into motion. But balancing on the rocking decks of his ship had made Erik quick and sure-footed. And accustomed to accessing men, he quickly recognized that Lord Frederick was swift and skilled but his lack of endurance was his Achilles heel. Capitalizing on his own stamina, Erik deliberately played cat and mouse with his opponent—he knew he had him!

Cool and calculating, Erik slowly drove his opponent into the far corner. And when he had nowhere to go, Erik closed in.

As Lord Frederick struggled to block the slashes of Erik's heavy blade, Erik momentarily gave in to his rage, goading him, "What's the matter; did you decide the lady's not worth fighting for?"

Up until now, Erik had channeled his fury into the fight, but as his opponent cowered, feebly begging for mercy, Erik let out an infuriated roar. "Well, I'll have you know—she's worth it to me!" In a decisive movement he rapidly drew down his sword, then turned his wrists and jerked the blade upward, catching his opponent's weapon from below. With one powerful lift of well-honed muscles, Erik sent Lord Frederick's sword flying.

In the next moment, it was all over. Erik felled his sniveling opponent with a single crushing blow.

But before he had even a moment to rejoice, frantic shouts echoed off the stone walls. "Fire! Fire!"

Erik shoved his sword in its scabbard, darted through the maze of stiff carcasses, and emerged into the courtyard.

A cannon shot had sparked a fire within the fortress and the wind rapidly whipped the flames into a frenzy that devoured everything in its path. Within minutes, acrid smoke poured up and out in black billows coupled with leaping scarlet flames that could be seen for miles—like a bloody gash in the early gray sky.

Fire and smoke snaked around the men engaged in combat inside the castle. Friend and foe alike, desperate to escape the flames, they swarmed up and over the walls. Sisal-rope scaling ladders were hastily dropped down the outside, and the men, choking and coughing, streamed down the wall.

Like the others driven by the smoke, Erik made his way up a stairwell, over the top of the wall, and then down a scaling ladder. Hampered by his armor, he was an easy target for an enemy archer on the ground. When a vengeful arrow caught him between his right leg-plates, he let out a yell and buckled forward, clinging desperately to the ropes as they swayed under the weight of moving men.

Olaf, directly below Erik on the ladder, saw the arrow pierce his flesh. With a shout to Erik to hold tight, he clenched his jaws and mustered every ounce of his strength to pull himself back up the several rungs separating them. Clinging to the ladder with one hand and swaying with it as men above and below continued to make their way down, Olaf used his free hand to seize the arrow sticking out of Erik's leg. He pulled it out with a decisive jerk.

The shock of the pain that tore through Erik temporarily disoriented him. He lost his grip. Down, down, he fell, crashing into the moat. Shouts went up from those soldiers who were close by, and several of them jumped into the water to pull their commander up the side and onto dry ground.

Erik clutched at his burning leg while he sputtered and spit out a mouthful of foul water. Karl pushed through the gathered crowd, unfastened Erik's leg plates and applied a dressing of salt and olive oil to the bloody, gaping wound. Then he wrapped a rude linen bandage around Erik's leg to hold the dressing in place.

Erik wasted no time in self-pity or regret. He cleared his lungs with a sharp cough, scraped the moisture off his face, sucked in a strong breath, and collected his wits. At his sharp whistle, his page appeared leading his mount and carrying his blue and white flag. The trumpeter dashed up behind him.

"Give me the banner. Sound a retreat," Erik shouted.

The page handed Erik the flag, and he waved it vigorously. The trumpeter raised his horn to his lips and blew a piercing blast. Instantly, Erik's men dropped back from pursuit and scrambled over fallen bodies to return to their original stations.

After a brief regrouping, Erik again signaled an attack. His men formed a circle and closed in on Lord Frederick's men. Those fortunate enough to still be alive now regretted their station outside the burning fortress as Erik's men fell with renewed vigor on those who tried to escape into the surrounding woods. Within an hour, dead bodies lay strewn all over the hillside surrounding Lord Frederick's fortress.

When the circle of men reached the burning fortress walls, their shouts rose in wave after wave of spontaneous loud cheering. Adding to the human cries, the trumpeter puffed out long, shrill blasts on his silver instrument. The men tending the food carts banged their metal utensils against the cooking pots, and two cannoneers shot off victory blasts.

As the swelling cacophony reverberated throughout the countryside, Erik's heart lurched with gratitude. He had done what he knew was right, God had fought for him in answer to his prayer, and he'd fulfilled his vow to his friend.

When the noise died down, Erik ordered the trumpeter to signal his men to return to their units. Following a head count, the unit commanders reported to Erik. God be praised, the months of training had paid off in *living* flesh. Only thirty-nine dead, one hundred twenty-three wounded, twelve missing. Each able man provided assistance for the suffering and did his duty by the dead.

Signs of scorching destruction floated in the air and a dreadful stench filled their nostrils as smoke continued to rise from the ruins. By the time everyone had reassembled, Lord Frederick's castle was a charred, shuddering shell that smoldered with the remains of its overly ambitious lord.

Gingerly, Erik swung his injured leg up and over his horse. When he was seated, he lifted his flag and signaled the trumpeter, who gave a final long and loud victory blast. The blue and white banner waved triumphantly, a bold silhouette against the setting sun as Eric rode the circuit of his men, congratulating them on a job well done.

# CHAPTER TEN

It was midmorning of the next day before Erik's army began moving. A slight breeze chased away the residual smoke from the still-smoldering shell of Lord Fredrick's fortress. The village men took the wounded with them, singing and shouting as they returned to their homes.

Erik's wounded leg throbbed like a bad tooth, but he knew a report to Lord Schmidden must come first before personal concerns. Leaving Olaf in charge of the slow-moving procession comprised of his men and all the battle equipment, Erik headed for Burg Mosel alone.

Anxious to share the good news with Lord Schmidden, he rode hard, arriving at Burg Mosel in the late afternoon. In the stable yard, he dismounted and threw the reins over his horse's head. Limping heavily, he crossed the yard and walked along the box hedge to the back door. Just inside the entrance hall, Erik jerked off his bulky leather vest and dropped it with a thud on the marble floor.

The jarring noise alerted Curtis to Erik's presence and he came to the doorway of his workroom. When Erik inquired where he might find Lord Schmidden, Curtis replied politely, "He's in the great room. He's been there since you left."

Motivated by his good news, Erik suppressed his pain and strode rapidly down the corridor. In the great room doorway he halted abruptly. Lord Schmidden, with his face buried in his hands, was kneeling by his carved chair. Erik hesitated, momentarily undecided as to whether he should interrupt the nobleman or quietly slip away and return later.

But Lord Schmidden had obviously been expecting Erik; his head came up and his deep voice welcomed Erik as he rose to his feet. "Come in, come in, my boy."

As Erik moved into the room, determinedly hiding his limp, Lord Schmidden met him and gripped him in a hearty embrace. Erik had mentally rehearsed the report he would make to Lord

Schmidden, but finding the man on his knees in prayer banished all thoughts of the battle.

"My lord, I do not mean to pry," Erik swallowed hard, "but Curtis said you have been there," he gestured toward Lord Schmidden's chair, "since I left."

The older man heaved a sigh. "Yes. I have been in prayer for your safe return and victory." Smiling now, "And it appears God has granted my request!"

"Yes, my lord. God has given us an amazing victory. Lord Frederick and Dagon are dead and the fortress is a burned-out shell!"

Tears welled up in Lord Schmidden's eyes. "Words are an empty way to pay my debt to you, but I am indeed grateful." He heaved a relieved sigh. "Now I can safely bring Rosamund home."

As the older man spoke his daughter's name, Erik couldn't help his telltale response: a flush that crept up his neck and suffused his face.

Nervously shifting his weight, Erik momentarily forgot his injured leg. At the sudden jolt of pain that shot through him, he grimaced and doubled over with a groan. Blood oozed out of the awkward bandage, trickled down his leg in rivulets, and dripped onto the marble floor.

Lord Schmidden instantly rang the bell pull, calling for help, and he offered Erik a room on the main floor in the west wing.

Erik vigorously resisted being treated like an invalid, but he finally agreed to place his arm across Lord Schmidden's shoulders for support, insisting he would be fine climbing the stairs to the tower room. With several servants following closely behind, he leaned on the older man and limped down the corridor, through the entrance hall, and past the chapel.

When they began the slow climb up the broad stairs toward his tower room, Erik halted every two or three steps, but halfway up the twenty-six steps, Erik's leg gave out. He fell heavily forward, clutching desperately at the stone wall for a handhold. His fingers scraped down the rough surface, shaving the skin off several knuckles, exposing raw flesh. Unable to get a grip and too weak to stop himself, Erik lunged sideways, his full weight slamming against the corner stone at the base of the thirteenth step. Pain tore through his shoulder. His ear and cheek burned from the impact.

Before Erik's body came to a stop, the wall made a rough, hollow, grinding sound. Lord Schmidden, thrown off balance by Erik's fall, thrust out his hand toward the wall to prevent his fall on top of Erik. The wall shuddered. Then a section of stones about two feet wide by four feet high and two feet thick slowly grated open.

Lord Schmidden fell into the opening with a crash. He landed on his stomach with his arm—the one he'd reached out to stop his fall—extended straight out along the floor above his head. As if pointing at something.

The servants took one look, turned and ran, tumbling and stumbling back down the stairs. Their hysterical shrieks were heard as far away as the scullery.

Erik clenched his teeth on a groan.

Lord Schmidden rolled over and sat up with his back to the opening. Slowly, painfully, Erik straightened up on the steps and swung around to face the older man. His eyes widened in shock, first at seeing the opening in the wall and then at the eerie spectacle illuminated by the glow from the stairwell candles.

"No!" came Erik's horror-filled cry.

Lord Schmidden leaned forward to offer his hand to help Erik up, exclaiming, "Branden, I'm so sorry." Seeing the consternation on Erik's face, Lord Schmidden shifted to turn his head to see what had upset Erik.

Sensing the older man's intent, Erik's hand shot out and he clutched Lord Schmidden's knee in a desperate grip. "Do not turn around," he commanded fiercely.

Waves of nausea swept over Erik. The pain in his leg and hand and shoulder and face were forgotten. He dropped his head between his knees and sucked in air in panting gulps.

"Oh, God, help!" he rasped as another wave of nausea rolled over him. Unconsciously, he continued squeezing Lord Schmidden's knee, as if by sheer force he could somehow prevent the older man from ever seeing the mysterious chamber's grim secret.

When the queasiness finally subsided, Erik slowly lifted his head. Maintaining his hold on Lord Schmidden's knee, he said gently. "Lord Schmidden, on the floor in the chamber behind you, there's a—a skeleton."

Lord Schmidden recoiled as if he'd been slapped. He leaped to his feet, sucking in a breath so loudly that Erik heard the gasp. And then he froze, immobilized by shock.

Horror swallowed them both.

Erik, fearing for Lord Schmidden's well being, pulled himself up to a standing position and placed a hand on the older man's shoulder. Without speaking, they turned and moved toward the skeleton. In the candlelight, the diamonds in the tiara glittered and the stones in the necklace, earrings and rings that lay in all the right places sparkled as though a tragedy had never taken place. And the remains of a satin dress gleamed in the low light.

"It's . . ." Lord Schmidden muffled his stricken whisper as he covered his pain-distorted face with a shaking hand. He moved nearer and bent down for a closer look. "Yes, it's Rose . . . and—and the baby." Raw emotion thinned his voice to a reedy pitch. "She'd just told me, that evening, that we were going to have a second child." He put out a hand and tentatively touched the remnants of the sleeve of the once-beautiful party dress.

Blackness engulfed Erik. He closed his eyes to

regain his composure, to momentarily shut out the older man's agony. His stomach resembled nothing so much as a fire ball in his gut. Words wouldn't come. What could he say?

Surprisingly, it was Lord Schmidden who regained his composure first. He straightened up and said gruffly, "Come, let's get you to your room." He grasped Erik's arm, raised it over his shoulder and aided him, one step at a time, to the landing outside Erik's tower room. He pushed open the door and they hobbled in together. Both in pain.

"I think I'll soak in the bath," Erik said, noticing steam rising from the copper tub waiting in front of the fireplace. He began stripping off his soiled clothing.

As the older man stumbled toward the door, Erik eyed him apprehensively. Would he be all right? Should he detain Lord Schmidden here where he could keep an eye on him? "Sir, what I really need is a clean bandage. There's one in my kit on the shelf." He pointed, "There. At the end."

When Lord Schmidden turned to locate the bandage, Erik carefully eased himself into the steaming water and wished he could thank whoever had built up the fire and filled the bath while he'd visited with Lord Schmidden. When the hot water hit his open wound, he stifled a sharp exclamation; it burned like fire. He pressed his lips together and grimaced as he gingerly fingered the torn flesh, but he was relieved to see that he was actually missing very little skin and the surrounding tissue was not red or inflamed. Karl's salt bandage had prevented the infection that could have developed from the foul water in the moat. A salve dressing, a good bandage, and a few days of inactivity would put the wound on the mend.

After Lord Schmidden deposited the clean bandage on the bed, he sank heavily into the nearby chair, buried his forehead in his palms, and groaned out loud. Because everything Erik could think of to say sounded trite, he said nothing and looked away out of respect and consideration.

Several minutes passed before Lord Schmidden raised his head. He straightened in the chair, stared at the wall, and began to talk out loud to God, quite as if he'd forgotten Erik's presence or his own whereabouts. "No one told me about a secret chamber. I always suspected there might be one, but we never found it." Despair edged his voice. "Rose must have fallen running up the steps. When the wall came open, she probably thought it would be a good joke to hide in there. She was a great one for pranks. I'm sure she never dreamed she couldn't get out, or that I wouldn't know how to get in. After all, my great-grandfather built the place and I've lived here all my life." His words held a bitter twist.

Erik wished he'd not been trapped into listening.

Lord Schmidden's tone change to resignation, "Well, God, You know best. She adored You, and I was the unfaithful one. Thank You for being so patient with my lack of trust. For being merciful—it could have been worse; her suffering ended quickly. Thank you for showing me what happened to her. And the child." He let his breath out in a harsh, ragged sigh as he rubbed his eyes and then wiped his hand over his face. "Now, at last, I can sleep in peace."

A low moan and another confession followed, as though further revelation had come to him. "Forgive me, God, for not teaching Rosamund about You." He clapped his hands to his temples. "I've failed miserably. I purposely shielded her from knowing about You. I thought if You couldn't take care of Rose,

I could do better than You, and Rosamund didn't need You. But I was wrong. Please, please God, forgive my foolish pride, for thinking I was wiser than You. Let me right the wrong I've done. Help me show her the way to You."

Erik, forgetting he was listening in on someone else's confession and that he'd resolved to keep his feelings about Rosamund to himself, impulsively blurted, "But Rosamund does know God."

Lord Schmidden's hands dropped to his knees and his head jerked around to confront Erik. Disbelief was plain on his face and his quietly controlled words pierced the air like daggers. "And just how would you know about Rosamund, Branden? I saw your face earlier when I mentioned her name." His eyes narrowed, "What haven't you told me?"

The time had come for Erik to bare his soul. And he did so bravely. Haltingly. He recounted his visit with Rosamund in Edith's cottage and related her memory of the night she lost her mother and of her discovery of the Book of Hours in her mother's chest, which had revealed God to her.

"And my lord," Erik stammered, "w-would you consider me as a suitor for your daughter ."

The silence that followed his request was so prolonged that Erik feared Lord Schmidden was considering how best to rebuke his impertinence. When the older man finally rose to his feet and swung around deliberately to confront him, Erik braced himself for disappointment.

Slowly nodding his head, Lord Schmidden declared gruffly, “I always wanted a son, and there’s no one I’d rather give Rosamund to, no one I’d rather see father my grandsons . . . pray with me . . . bury me.” He threw back his shoulders, once again a man in charge. “You have my wholehearted blessing. Consider the matter settled.”

Hope surged in Erik’s heart at that first word, “son,” and he struggled to control the tumult that shook him, but after clearing his throat, he found his voice. “Thank you, my lord.” He hesitated, then blurted a final request, “Would you please not tell Rosamund? I’d like the chance to win her heart.” Erik looked away, embarrassed to be discussing his tender affection.

Lord Schmidden ran his long fingers through his silvery-white hair. “I’ll be making the burial arrangements for Rose in the morning, and then I’ll see what I can do about fetching a certain young woman." His eyes twinkled. "And you have my word; I'll let you do the talking."

His smile was so warm and open that Erik couldn't help grinning back. "Thank you, my lord!" The appropriate words seemed so inadequate.

Lord Schmidden headed toward the door then turned to say over his shoulder, "Let's hope "my lord" will soon be "Papa."

That last word of acceptance erased the final vestiges of Erik's fear, but his heart ached for his friend when he heard him marching bravely down the steps to deal with the hard reality of Rose's tragic death. *God tests all men's hearts,* he thought. *One day my turn will come.*

June 1, 1423. Burg Mosel.

## CHAPTER ELEVEN

Early evening shadows flowed over the castle garden in swirling purple and blue tints that reminded him of a bishop's moiré silk cassock. Wispy white clouds scudded across the sky as the sun, dropping down to hug the distant mountains, prepared to end the day's work. Blooming roses shared their fragrant offering, and somewhere in the soft gloaming a rusty-headed little hawfinch sang his evensong. The white marble garden bench, cornered into a cool sanctuary of forest green, held a solitary worshipper.

Erik soaked up the last of the sun's healing rays, observed the time on the nearby sundial, and let his gaze drift over the rose garden. A buzzing bee caught his attention and he watched it drift from flower to flower. Had it really only been a week since their victory over Lord Frederick and the discovery of the secret chamber?

Four days ago he'd divided his crew into two units. Olaf and those men choosing to return to Sweden via Denmark had departed three days ago, while those desiring to connect with the trade route to seek sea passage back to Sweden had set off with Karl yesterday. Erik had assigned rights to The Tarragon, whatever its state of disrepair, to Olaf without a single regretful twinge. His ship and the adventures it represented seemed to belong to another lifetime.

He'd discovered that the pain of a puncture wound is not limited to the actual injury site. In fact, his hip had caused him more discomfort than the actual wound. He still found himself favoring his right leg, but the aching had diminished and he felt sure he would soon be as fit as ever.

Lord Schmidden sent a messenger to King Sigismund, informing him of the outcome of this local skirmish and advising him of Erik's role in the victory. He confided to Erik his hope that a title might be bestowed upon Erik as reward for his valiant heroism, stating that the king was generous in conferring honor, however reluctant he might be to get involved in local disputes.

Lord Schmidden had also invited Erik to accompany him in riding over the newly acquired property, promising they would do that next week. The realization that it would all one day be his humbled him. A home and a family—and not just any family, but one with such a noble heritage—was more than he could have imagined. His heart swelled with gratitude.

And Rosamund. Her father had gone to fetch her and she would be home tomorrow. Erik found it difficult to concentrate for long on anything else.

Pensive, he considered the plans for the interment of Rose Schmidden and her unborn child. A casket had been prepared and Father Andrew had agreed to officiate, but the ceremony would wait until Rosamund could be present. Erik knew Lord Schmidden planned to tell Rosamund about everything that had happened during her absence before they arrived back at Burg Mosel.

After thoroughly investigating the secret chamber, Lord Schmidden talked of sealing it shut. However, following a night of prayer and a consultation with Father Andrew, he decided that leaving it open would serve as a reminder of his renewed consecration and trust in God. Erik admired Lord Schmidden for his brave decision.

Over the past week the grieving man had often fallen silent, a sad expression filling his eyes, and although Erik had noticed the nobleman's melancholy, he'd hesitated to say anything. Then as they sat by the fire one evening, Lord Schmidden had spoken about the tragedy.

"In my rejection of God I was a lot worse off than Rose. There was so little air in that chamber, she just went to sleep. I doubt she felt any pain. But my spiritual death was far more slow and agonizing. Deciding to eliminate God wasn't the end; it was just the beginning. Pride led to a slow death; it crept in and cut off circulation one limb at a time, squeezing the life out of me, bit by bit." He grimaced. "Bitterness is a foul-smelling puss that only God can cleanse."

He wiped his hand over his face, as if to erase the past. "And my greatest sorrow is not Rose's death, although I've missed her terribly, missed the fulfillment of all we hoped to share, missed the child we would have had. No, my greatest regret is the years without the friendship of God. Life is a suffocating business without Him."

While Erik sat on the garden bench, lost in reflection, the sun dropped below the horizon. A sudden, cool breeze prompted him to stand and stretch his tall frame to full height. Still contemplative, he followed the rose-bordered cobbled walkway through the courtyard and entered the arched wooden back doors that opened into the vaulted main hallway.

As he headed toward the tower stairs, he stopped in surprise. The heavy chains declaring the chapel off-limits were gone. He'd entertained curiosity about the sanctuary because of Rosamund's reference to sensing God's presence there, but chains had barred the doors. One of the servants must have removed them while he was in the garden.

Feeling a sense of awe, Erik approached the doors and pushed one open. As he stepped inside, he instinctively looked around for the font of holy water. The milky white scalloped marble basin with an overlooking cherub rested in a niche in the wall by the door, but when he reached in, he found it dry.

He offered a brief bow of respect to

acknowledge Christ's presence before he looked around, noting the simple wooden prie dieux that stood at right angles along the outer walls and formed a center aisle where the polished parquet floor shone with a high gloss. Arched beams supported the walls at intervals and shouldered the graceful dome. The Good Shepherd, depicted in brilliant color in the stained glass window, provided the room's only source of light—and He was every bit as embracing as Rosamund had implied.

As he gazed at the window, the Shepherd's eyes seemed to draw him, and his heart responded. He made his way up to the altar railing and knelt. Fading daylight glowed through the window and cast an other-worldly radiance upon his face. As he bowed in prayer, he sensed God's mysterious presence, the same protecting Presence he'd felt when looking up at the stars that first night of his journey to this place.

When he rose to leave, the burial chamber in the left transept—an ante-room opening off the nave and filling the empty space beneath the tower stairs—caught his attention. The ceiling was low, and words inscribed on the soffit above the compartment stated: *"God is not the God of the dead, but of the living."*

Just inside the chamber doorway a large, leather-bound book lay open on a lectern. His curiosity piqued, he moved close and scanned the last several entries:

*June 5, 1398 Nicklaus Schmidden and*
*Rose Marie Glinden, Holy Matrimony*
*August 12, 1402 Leopold Schmidden*
*Death, plague*
*August 27, 1402 Clara Brunnell Schmidden*
*Death, plague*
*July 15, 1403 Rosamund Jeanne Schmidden*
*Birth. Daughter of Nicklaus and*
*Rose Glinden Schmidden*

Reading the names and dates, it occurred to Erik that no final entry had been made for Rosamund's mother. He knew the sadness he felt could in no way compare to the talons of painful uncertainty that surely clawed at those who knew and loved her.

He swallowed hard over the lump in his throat and sniffed in the stale smell of cold, dry stone as he approached the coffins. They were stacked four high and only the front end of each was visible. Some were very old, and the names etched in the stone were barely distinguishable. With his finger he traced the faint markings on those in the first row: Alfred,

Gunter, Lisle. Then the second row: Nicklaus, Elsa, Leopold, Clara. Smaller caskets, obviously children's, stood beside them: Frances, Rolf, Margaret, Anna, Heinrich, Harold, Henrietta.

And soon there would be another. Rose Schmidden. Life was certainly fragile and to be treasured.

Erik stepped back into the chapel and looked up again at the words inscribed above the chamber, ". . . God of the living," and he reflected on the freedom physical death brings to those who know God. Resting in those burial containers were only the physical remains of people whose spirits had been released from the restraint of time to join God in eternity. There are always those who go before and those who follow after, and he felt a sense of duty to uphold the honor of those who'd gone before him and to pass on an untarnished birthright to those who would follow him.

Erik hesitated at the chapel doors, casting one final glance around the sanctuary. Darkness, rather than smothering the room, served only to intensify the jeweled colors of the stained glass Shepherd, the representation of Christ that had watched over the members of this family for over a hundred years. A surge of anticipation gripped him as he thought about becoming a part of Rosamund's family, and if God should graciously allow, future generations.

Erik slipped out and closed the chapel doors. Forgetting his injury, he took the stone stairs two at a time.

June 2, 1423. Altwarp, Pomerania.

## CHAPTER TWELVE

Rosamund walked along the shore near Edith's cottage for the last time. Sultry nuances of salt water and seaweed carried on the gentle breeze caressed her skin and hair as she thought back to the frightened girl she'd been when she'd come to stay with Edith. She licked the salty sea spray from her lips and reflected on how her world had changed in the past five months. And now Papa had come for her and she was going home.

Last night he had shared the news surrounding her mother's death and that of their unborn child. As the three of them wept, Edith hugged them tightly in her shaking arms, steadied her quavering voice, and whispered comforting words, "I'll be tellin' Rose 'hello' for ye, I will. She be waitin' for me, I mind. Now that I be done servin' my purpose, I 'spect to soon be departin' in peace." So they put away their grief like a keepsake in the jewel boxes of their hearts.

Intuitively aware that they would never be together again on this earth, they cherished each moment, eating and laughing and listening as Lord Schmidden told of Erik's miraculous march across the frozen sea, his subsequent conquest of Lord Frederick, and his injured leg.

Rosamund gasped when her father spoke of Erik's injury and then coughed to cover her dismay. She missed the shrewd glance her father sent her way, and when he continued speaking, relating battle details, her silence told its own story.

Restless and anxious to be going home, Rosamund had risen early and dressed quickly in the least worn of Kathe's *cottes*. With a twinge of regret she'd wished for one of her own attractive gowns even as she recognized that Kathe's homespun would certainly be more suitable for the long journey ahead.

"Rosamund! It's time."

Responding to her father's call, Rosamund returned to Edith's cottage, where tears and hugs accompanied her heartfelt good-bye before she joined her father in the carriage.

Happy to be together, father and daughter rode for several hours in near silence. Three times Lord Schmidden tried to find the right words to tell Rosamund of his renewed commitment to God, but each time he tried to frame his thoughts into words, he couldn't seem to get past Erik's revelation that she'd encountered God for herself. Not wanting to betray Erik's confidence, even inadvertently, he finally resolved to say nothing and wait, hoping his daughter would make a comment that would provide him the desired opportunity.

Rosamund mentioned details of her stay at Edith's, elaborating on the comfort she'd found in the special book, his gift to her mother.

Her openness provided the opportunity for Lord Schmidden to express his heart. "I, too, have come back to God. He gave me a long leash but He never let me go. And He's been faithful to me in spite of my failure to trust Him." Regret roughened his voice. "Forgive me for failing you, too."

Rosamund covered her father's fist that was clenched on his knee next to hers with her slender white hand and leaned her head on his shoulder. "Papa, there's nothing to forgive," she whispered.

"God has filled the emptiness in my heart and taken away the pain."

He slipped his arm around her shoulders and they rode in silence, their love for each other deep and strong.

After a while, from a drowsy distance, Rosamund broke the peaceful silence, "Papa?" When he nodded and raised his bushy brows to indicate she had his attention, she continued, "Did a man ever live at Burg Mosel who taught my mother to play the harpsichord?"

"Pierre. Pierre Monet." He said the name slowly, tentatively. "I haven't thought of him in years." He questioned her in surprise, "You don't remember him?" Then shaking his head he answered himself, "No, of course you wouldn't, you weren't born yet. He lived with us at Burg Mosel for about a year soon after we were married. He came back occasionally to visit after he left. Come to think of it, he came for Josie's wedding. I guess that's the last time we ever saw him. I wonder what became of him."

"And he taught my mother to play the harpsichord?"

"Yes." He drew his lips into a straight,

disapproving line. "Quite the young stag, he was. He had all the maids swooning over him, although he didn't give them a second glance. I didn't relish his company; his melancholy streak was a bit much for me, but Rose knew him quite well, of course."

Lord Schmidden paused, his brows descending over thoughtful eyes before he turned his head to inquire, "Why did you ask?"

Rosamund wasn't quite sure what to make of Edith's odd remark about the man who'd "made eyes" at her mother, but not wishing to rouse any question as to the reason for her curiosity, she responded to her father in a drowsy, disinterested tone, "Hmm? Oh, Edith mentioned him." She would think about it later.

With a lazy stretch she sat up and deliberately moved the conversation into a brighter vein. "Papa, is Erik's crew still at Burg Mosel?" It was an indirect way to ask about Erik, but she couldn't quite bring herself to inquire straight out.

"No, they're gone. They separated into two groups and set off for Sweden several days ago.

Rosamund's heart sank. What else was there to say? Erik was gone.

When Burg Mosel came into view, proud and

grand with its bright blue banner waving a welcome in the late afternoon sunshine, Rosamund became restless. She'd missed her home. And Kathe. And Pfeffer.

As the carriage passed through the gate, she clutched her father's sleeve. Her face was flushed and her eyes sparkled with excitement. She stood up almost before they'd come to a stop and was out of the carriage and fairly flying up the long flight of steps. She flashed through the front doors like a streak of lightning. Rushing through the main entrance hallway, she nodded to her ancestors on either side as she whizzed by. She laughed softly to herself; they didn't look at all like the glowering faces she'd left behind.

Hastily plunging down the back stairs to the scullery, Rosamund's feet slid out from under her. With a rude thud she bumped to an inglorious stop on the cold stones. Stunned, she sat there for a minute.

"Rosamund, sometimes you're so impulsive. When will you act like a lady?" she laughingly chided herself under her breath, undaunted by the spill.

Then her mouth dropped open. It couldn't be

happening again. But it was. The conversation taking place in the scullery, which she couldn't help overhearing, made her heart constrict. "I wonder how Miss Rosamund will like finding herself the prize for winning her papa's war."

Rosamund's head snapped up, her eyes narrowed, and a frown distorted her face. Herself a prize. Whose prize? And who was that, gossiping, anyway?

Then she heard Hilde's familiar voice, "How came you by this notion, Letty?"

So it *was* Letty. She never had trusted the cook.

Rosamund could almost hear Letty's smirk. "Matilda and I went back up the stairs after Lord Schmidden and Master Erik found Lady Rose's bones in that there chamber. The men were in the tower room and they left the door open and I heard Lord Schmidden sayin' the marriage was set." She didn't bother with a breath. "I'd have heard more, too, but Matilda pulled me away 'cause she was afraid we'd be caught eavesdropping." Rosamund heard a loud bang, as if Letty slammed down a kettle to emphasize her statement. "There now, do you doubt my word?"

Angry and humiliated, Rosamund leaped to her

feet. Without stopping to think, she burst through the doorway. Heads jerked. Guilty faces blanched. Several astonished maids dropped what they were doing. A kettle splashed into a pan filled with water. A crockery bowl smashed to bits on the stone floor.

Pairs of horrified eyes riveted on Lord Schmidden's daughter. Lady Rosamund—here? Of course the servants talked about the nobility they served, but it was considered shameful to be caught. And Rosamund had heard their indiscretion; there could be no doubt.

"For shame! I shall speak to Papa about this. Clean up that mess," she pointed an accusing finger at the shattered shards, "and see to it you mind your own business." Her words scorched and her blue eyes threw out angry sparks.

She fled back up the stairs and out the back door. What a welcome home!

Rosamund rushed along the hedge and darted across the stable yard, her flying feet spraying gravel in her wake. She pushed open the door to the stable, inhaled the musty barn smell mingled with that of straw and oats, and flew past the stalls and pens.

Forgetting her *cotte* and ignoring the gate, she

scrambled between the bars into Pfeffer's pen, flung herself against him and wrapped her arms around his neck. He turned his head toward her nickering a welcome. "Dear old Pfeffer. You're my faithful friend," she cried.

Her mind raced. Letty said Erik was going to marry her. Excitement sent a sent a flush over her whole body before her reason said: But how could that be? Papa said Erik's crew had gone.

Her momentary joy dissolved and the scullery conversation she'd overheard resurfaced, twisting her emotions yet again.

Betrayal! How could Papa offer her as a prize for winning his war?

Anger! How could Erik agree to such a bargain?

Insult! How could Letty repeat such gossip?

Frustration! Why did it hurt so badly to think Erik and Papa had disposed of her future without consulting her?

Shock! She *loved* Erik. That's why it hurt.

A low moan escaped her lips as the truth hit her so hard that her legs wobbled: all these years she had cared for someone who could coldly decide she would be an adequate reward. First, Lord Frederick's villainous betrayal, and now this. Oh, her foolish heart!

Shaking with wild sobs, she sank to the floor in Pfeffer's pen. Grabbing up handfuls of straw, she flicked it into the air in angry jerks. Her cheeks burned and the laces down the back of Kathe's old *cotte* seemed much too tight; she could hardly breathe.

Pfeffer nickered softly and nuzzled up to her, nudging her to a sitting position. She sniffled, dried her eyes on her sleeve, and hiccupped.

A familiar deep voice spoke softly from somewhere near the railing. "Lady Rosamund, are you unwell?"

Erik?

Rosamund was on her feet in an instant. What was he doing here? How long had he been standing there?

Fury mingled with embarrassment. "You! How could you?" she burst out. Revenge swelled up within her and her narrowed eyes turned black. She grabbed the nearest object, a bucket. Thinking to fling its liquid contents on Erik, she heaved it toward him. She knew in an instant that later she would regret losing the last of her dignity, but for the moment it felt intensely satisfying.

It wasn't water!

Shock threatened to overcome her as the air mushroomed with a thick cloud of Pfeffer's ground oats. And worse, Erik dodged. Scratchy particles caught in her nose and throat, and she gagged on the feed dust, coughing and choking uncontrollably. Tears ran down her face.

Was he laughing at her?

She glared at him, glared at the empty bucket still clutched in her hot fist, glared again at an astounded, wide-eyed Erik. Infuriated at her failure to execute revenge, she gritted her teeth and ground out in exasperation, "Rrrr."

Taken by surprise, Erik stared at her. But his speechlessness only magnified her mortification. Flustered and enraged, she pitched the empty bucket into the corner, jerked open the gate to Pfeffer's pen, and stormed, still fuming, out of the stable.

She fled across the stable yard and along the length of the hedge toward the back doors. Her eyes stung with tears; whether of anger, shame, humiliation, or disappointment, she didn't quite know. And all the while she muttered threats of vengeance beneath her breath. She twitched her skirt roughly when it caught on something—she didn't bother to see what, and she yanked it free, almost relishing the ripping sound that followed.

She clutched her torn skirt with both hands and pounded up the stairs and along the corridor to her own room. With a vicious thrust she slammed the door behind her. Sobbing wildly, she flung herself on her bed and pounded her fists into the white duvet. At last, disconsolate and exhausted, Rosamund curled up in the middle of her bed.

Gradually, as the gentle peace and familiarity of her own room massaged her hurt feelings, she began to relax. Her gaze perused the room. Everything was just as she had left it.

Leaning up on one elbow, Rosamund's eyes fell on her trunk and her mother's chest that the servants had carried up for her. Acting on a sudden urgent impulse, she slid off the bed and fell to her knees in front of the chest. Her frantic fingers struggled with the latch.

When she finally held the Book of Hours in her hands, she clasped it tightly to her heart and moved to sit on the edge of the bed. The words of this book had given her comfort before. Maybe God could help her think clearly about her new distress.

She laid the book face down on the bed, unfastened the clasp, and opened it from the back. She did not want to see that yellow rose today. And she didn't want to consider why she felt that way.

Using her thumb, she carefully flipped the pages and stopped at *Hour Fourteen.*

*O thou my God, save thy servant*
*That trusteth in thee.*
*Be merciful unto me, O Lord:*
*For I cry unto thee daily.*
*Rejoice the soul of thy servant:*
*For unto thee, O Lord, do I lift up my soul.*
*For thou, Lord, art good, and ready to forgive;*
*And plenteous in mercy*
*Unto all them that call upon thee:*
*For thou wilt answer me.*
*Teach me thy way, O Lord;*
*I will walk in thy truth . . .*

As if her own heart had written the words, she personalized them. "Save me, Your servant who trusts in You . . . Bring joy to my heart . . . I am so glad You're forgiving and good . . . Be my Teacher so I will walk in Your truth."

Rosamund closed the volume, refastened the clasp, and lifted the book to rest against her chest.

Lying back on the bed, she stared at the walnut candle stand embellished with carved vines and leaves that held candles for illuminating the night, her anger dissipated. It really didn't matter what Papa and Erik had done. She was only responsible for herself. And she knew she was wrong on two counts. She had assumed Letty's gossip was true, and she had lost her temper and behaved shamefully.

She swallowed hard at the thought of apologizing. However, not one to remain idle once a decision was made, Rosamund jumped to her feet and scurried across the navy and cream wool rug that covered the wood floor between the bed and the fireplace.

Screened behind the room divider that provided privacy for dressing, she ripped off the torn *cotte* and tossed it over her shoulder; it landed in a crumpled heap on the floor near the fireplace. Choosing one of her own garments, the turquoise blue silk, she pulled it over her head, smoothed it over her kirtle, and cinched up the laces. There was no time to wait for assistance today.

She scuffed off her heavy shoes and located a pair of soft leather slippers.

On a sudden impulse, she dropped to her knees beside her mother's chest. Pressing her index finger against the catch, she released the spring and raised the top. Taking up the small wooden box that held her mother's pearl earrings, she slid open the lid and retrieved the jewels. When she'd screwed them in place on her ears, she dropped the box back into the chest.

Moving to the dressing table, she sat on her curved-back chair and picked up her brush. When a vigorous brushing of her disheveled hair sent wisps of straw floating to the floor, she cringed in dismay; she must have looked like a barnyard fowl to Erik! Embarrassment burned her cheeks and made her brush even harder.

When she'd twisted her hair up and back and fastened it in a mature, sophisticated style—most unlike her recent behavior, she muttered, "If I must eat humble pie, perhaps looking pretty will help it taste better."

She rinsed her face and hands with water from the pitcher on the bedside table and dried them with the linen towel stitched with dainty blue flowers along one edge that lay waiting for her use.

Catching up a peacock plume from her dressing table, she twitched it nervously to cool her cheeks. Determination tightened her lips into a straight line; she would go talk to Papa.

## CHAPTER THIRTEEN

The situation appeared quite different from Erik's perspective. While visiting Curtis in his small front workroom, Erik saw Rosamund flash past the doorway as she darted for the stairs. With great effort he replied to Curtis's question about the state of his injury; he didn't wish to be rude or to reveal the sudden pounding in his chest, but he quickly ended the conversation as politely as possible and turned to leave.

However, when he heard echoing footsteps rushing back up the scullery stairs, he stopped in the doorway. He watched Rosamund dash for the back door and he heard the thud as it slammed shut.

Erik followed her, stepping outside in time to see her disappear into the stable. He crossed the yard and pushed open the heavy stable door. A low moan sent alarm skittering along his veins. He rushed toward the far end of the stable, but Rosamund's hysterical weeping was echoing in the rafters by the time he reached her.

He stopped outside Pfeffer's pen and watched her sink to the straw in an agitated heap. Girls and their tears were not easy for Erik to understand, and he felt perplexed and helpless. Crossing his arms on the rails, he waited, casting about in his mind for something appropriate to say.

When her weep-fest subsided, Rosamund sat up. Dabbing at her tearstained face, she left streaks and smudges on her cheeks and chin. Despite her distress, a halo of golden straw frosted her dark hair; she looked like an angel to Erik.

Unaware he played a role in her anguish, he gently questioned, "Lady Rosamund, are you unwell?"

Leaping to her feet, sending straw flying, she struck out at him like an angry brooding hen. "You! How could you?"

Her violent reaction left him speechless.

In the next moment, she reached down for the nearby feed bucket. Reading malicious intent in her eyes, he sidestepped the oncoming cloud of grain—and caught her glare at his unscathed condition.

She eyed the now empty feed bucket and then looked back to him, and although he perceived her chagrin at her backfired efforts, he remained paralyzed, stunned by her ill-tempered behavior. What had become of the perfect girl of his dreams? He rubbed a hand over his face, struggling with shock and disbelief.

Rosamund stomped her foot, emitting angry growls as she flung the bucket into the corner. She jerked open the gate to Pfeffer's pen, shoved past Erik, and fled out of the stable.

With movements that were more automatic than deliberate, Erik closed the swinging gate to Pfeffer's pen and leaned against it, trying to clear his mind. Then resolve turned him on his heel, and he followed Rosamund out of the stable.

When Erik spotted Lord Schmidden speaking with Curtis in the entrance hall, he interrupted them, his voice strained and his face wearing his tension. "My lord, I need to speak to you at once. I'll be in the great room." He turned abruptly, not waiting for Lord Schmidden to respond.

Quickly excusing himself to his clerk, Lord Schmidden followed Erik to the great room.

Emptied of all signs of military engagement, the room reflected its former elegance. The two heavily carved chairs and the little stool were once again in their familiar positions by the fire. Lord Schmidden motioned Erik to be seated and settled into his own chair. One bushy eyebrow quirked up as Rosamund's father inquired, "Now then, what's on your mind, Branden?"

Erik stammered and stumbled over his words while Lord Schmidden regarded him in keen surprise. "Well, my lord," Erik scratched his head, "I don't know exactly." Nearly incoherent, Erik cleared his throat and began again. "At least, I mean, why is she so angry?" He threw out his hands in confused desperation. "What is it I'm supposed to have done?"

Lord Schmidden did not smile, but his blue eyes under their brooding brows twinkled with amusement that Erik Branden could lead an army to victory but in matters of the heart he couldn't see for the fog.

"Assuming *her* is Rosamund, what did you say to her?" he probed patiently.

Frustration crossed Erik's face. "That's just it. I don't know."

Lord Schmidden raised his bushy brows. “What do you mean, you don’t know?”

“Well, my lord, when I saw how upset—”

“Upset?” Lord Schmidden interrupted sharply.

“Why, yes. I asked her if she was unwell.”

“Unwell? Why would she be unwell?” Lord Schmidden eyes narrowed as he pinched his lower lip.

“That’s the problem. I don’t know.”

Lord Schmidden cleared his throat and resisted the temptation to roll his eyes. “Let’s back up. Where did you first see Rosamund?”

Erik enunciated each syllable slowly and clearly. “She rushed through the front doors and headed down the scullery stairs.”

“Did you follow her?”

“No, not then.”

“All right. Then what happened?”

“In a few minutes she ran back up the stairs and rushed out the back door.”

“Hmm. And where were you?”

“Speaking with Curtis, my lord. We were in his workroom.”

“I see. And then?”

"I excused myself and followed her."

"Where did she go?"

"To the stable, my lord."

Lord Schmidden nodded. "Did you go after her?"

"Yes. But she didn't see me."

"Oh. And why is that?" His eyes narrowed. "Didn't you want her to see you?"

"No, my lord. At least, that is—not right away."

Lord Schmidden drew down his heavy brows and growled, "And why not?"

"Well, because she was crying in the horse pen."

Gripping the chair arms and halfway rising out of the seat, Lord Schmidden exclaimed, "Crying in the horse pen!" He sank back in his chair, his fingers squeezing the lion paws on the ends of the chair arms.

Erik sighed, his shoulders slumping. "Yes, my lord. So I asked if she was unwell. I wanted to help."

Lord Schmidden relaxed his grip on the chair and splayed his fingers. "And?" Eyes on his hands, he repeated the finger stretching movement.

"Well, she seemed shocked to see me, my lord. Didn't she know I was here?" His blue gaze bored into the older gentleman's eyes.

Lord Schmidden looked thoughtful for a moment. "Come to think of it, I guess I didn't tell her." He took a deep breath and remarked in a puzzled tone, "But that shouldn't have upset her enough to make her cry. I got a strong impression that she likes you."

Erik stiffened. "Well, I doubt it. She threw a bucketful of feed at me."

"She *what*?" Lord Schmidden barked. His face twitched as he struggled to get himself under control. He leaned his elbows on the chair arms and pressed his fingertips together, demanding, "Didn't she *say* anything?"

Erik, now totally exasperated, shot back, "Well, yes, she said something like, 'How could you?' She was terribly upset, my lord." His tone grew defensive, "And I was shocked by her outrageous behavior."

"And what is it she thinks you've done?"

Erik's head reared back and his hands curled into fists. "That's just it; I don't know, my lord. She ran out of the stable." He stopped short, adding as an afterthought, "I didn't know what to think—so I came to you." Then almost under his breath, as though talking to himself, he lowered his head and added with a groan, "She's so beautiful." He passed a shaking hand over his eyes.

In spite of his obvious concern, Lord Schmidden stifled a chuckle before he suggested, "Well, my boy, the best thing you can do is talk to her."

"I don't want to talk to her. She has a beastly temper," Erik snapped, grappling with disillusionment. His angel was flesh and blood.

Lord Schmidden rose to his feet, agreeing, "You're right. *I'll* talk to her. Now, you just lean back and relax for a few minutes. We'll get this all straightened out in no time." His tone was both conciliatory and indulgent. He moved to the sideboard, where he filled a goblet with honeyed mead and handed it to Erik.

While Lord Schmidden paced, Erik gulped his drink, desperately trying to believe everything would work out.

* * *

Lord Schmidden stifled his inopportune mirth. Life would never be dull for these two if today held any portent of the future. He had almost resolved to go looking for his daughter when he heard her soft footfalls in the corridor. The steps came closer, and in the next moment she moved into the room, as beautiful in his eyes as Esther, the biblical queen.

Lost in his own thoughts, his head leaning on his hand and his eyes closed, Erik missed Rosamund's entrance.

But she saw him.

She froze for a moment and then fluttered as if she were a bird about to take flight to escape.

Lord Schmidden spoke quickly to forestall further conflict, "Come in, Rosamund. It seems you and I need to have a talk."

He turned to Erik, who by now had his eyes open and was staring, transfixed. "Would you please excuse us, Branden? Why don't you wait for us in the garden?"

Erik rose to leave, his gaze still fastened on Rosamund. She, on the other hand, refused to meet his penetrating blue eyes.

As soon as Erik moved out of earshot, Rosamund started to protest that she wasn't sure she wanted to join Erik later—in the garden or, for that matter, anywhere at all.

But again, Lord Schmidden spoke first. "Come here, my dear." He caught her hand and drew her onto his knee as he sat in his chair. "Now, come, my dear; tell your Papa all about it?" he invited in a disarming tone.

She drew in a ragged breath and pinched the feathers on the peacock plume. Finally, she lifted her head and said reproachfully, "Papa, how could you?"

Lord Schmidden shook his head, and if he hadn't thought he might further damage Rosamund's already injured feelings, he would have laughed out loud. But instead he gently turned her chin so she had to look into his eyes. "How could I do what?"

The pitch of her voice went up several degrees and tears threatened to spill down her cheeks. "Pa-pa! How could you promise to give me to Erik as a reward for winning your stupid war?"

Lord Schmidden smothered his smile as he watched Rosamund swallow hard and clutch desperately at her shredded dignity. What had been so important was now irrelevant!

Gently patting her shoulder, he voiced his dawning comprehension. "Is that what this is all about?" His eyes narrowed. "Don't you like Erik?"

"Why, yes, but—" She stopped abruptly and bit her lip. Her face flushed at her bold admission.

"But what?" *Aha! Now I'm getting somewhere,* he thought, raising one eyebrow quizzically.

"Well, I want him to like me for me, and not because . . ." she buried her words along with her blush against Papa's shoulder.

After a reassuring hug, Lord Schmidden held her away from his chest, lifted her chin, and smoothed her dark hair away from her forehead. "Rosamund, Rosamund," he whispered her name affectionately before explaining, "offering you as a reward for winning the war was never part of my discussion with Erik." His arms tightened around her. "Erik cares for you, and I gave him permission to ask you to marry him."

Rosamund's hunched figure straightened and she leaned away from her father so hastily she nearly slipped from her perch on his knee. Her dewy eyes brightened with hope. "Really, Papa? Did you—does he *really*?"

"Well, let me put it this way; I think that's something he is hoping to tell you himself," Lord Schmidden evaded her question with an indulgent smile.

She jumped to her feet. "I must go apologize. I

treated him shamefully, Papa." Chagrin mingled with pride and mischief on her face.

Lord Schmidden nodded as he said dryly, "I know all about it."

Not halfway to the door, she stopped. Hesitated. Looked back. She twitched the feather plume in her restless fingers. "You don't think he'll have changed his mind, do you? I did behave dreadfully, Papa." Worry furrowed her brow and she chewed on her lower lip.

Lord Schmidden's eyes danced, but he disciplined the grin that tugged once again at the corners of his mouth as he reassured her, "No, my dear, I'm sure he won't change his mind."

She ran back to him, bent down and planted a quick kiss on his cheek, and then disappeared out the door.

Lord Schmidden watched her go, his shoulders shaking with his silent chuckles; he hadn't had such a good laugh in a long time.

## CHAPTER FOURTEEN

Completely forgetting her earlier intention to be dignified, Rosamund rushed to the castle garden. When she didn't immediately see Erik, she froze in sudden panic. Where was he? Maybe Papa was wrong after all. Oh, he couldn't be. He just couldn't be. "Please, God," she muttered a frantic prayer.

Her heart almost stopped beating when she spotted him. His back to her and frustration written in every line of his body, Erik paced back and forth in front of the stone bench. Preoccupied, he didn't hear her approach.

Feeling suddenly shy, Rosamund summoned all her courage and softly called his name, "Erik."

The cords in his neck bulged, but he continued pacing.

Despite the fear spiraling through her, Rosamund smothered her apprehensions and valiantly refused to give in to the desire to run away as fast and as far as possible. Bravely, she repeated his name, "Erik?" This time her tone carried question and apology.

He turned slowly, eyeing her with a mixture of hurt and hope.

She dropped her head and stared at her slender fingers, fingers that were very busy smoothing her peacock feather. She bit her lips to control their quivering. Her long lashes brushed her white cheeks. Tormented. Tormenting.

"What is it you think I've done?" Erik's anguished words defined the space between them.

Rosamund's heart tripped up her vocal chords and her words came out in a meek little squeak. "I overheard Letty," she gave the feather plume a diffident twitch, "say that I was to be your prize for winning Papa's war." Her chin was as far down as it could go and scarlet mortification spread to her widow's peak. She poked at the cobblestones in the walkway with the toe of her slipper.

When Erik didn't speak, Rosamund ever-so-slowly lifted her lashes to peek up at him.

A hurt-little-boy look lurked in his eyes as they

met hers, and his mouth twisted painfully with each word, "I'm sorry you would have minded if that were true."

Erik's misunderstanding snapped the bands of fear that had squeezed her heart. She stepped close to him and clasped his arm, protesting earnestly, "But I wouldn't have minded at all."

Erik jerked free from her grasp. "Don't tease me, Rosamund." He swung away from her, exclaiming harshly, "I-I want your love, not your pity."

"I do feel love for you," she announced desperately. "I came here to apologize for losing my temper and behaving abominably."

His back was as formidable as the stone tower at Feste Burg.

She tried again, "Papa said you'd forgive me. Oh, please, you will, won't you?" She swallowed a frantic cry. *Oh, God, help me control my tongue from this day forward!*

Erik hesitated then stopped.

Rosamund held her breath.

Gripping the hem of his *tabard* with white-knuckled fingers, Erik whipped around to face her.

"Do you even know what you're saying?"

Rosamund answered boldly, "Yes, I do." She lifted her chin and smiled up at him. "I love you, Erik Branden."

"Rosamund!" He took a step toward her and opened his arms.

She went straight into them, wrapping her arms around his back as he pressed tender kisses on her shining crown of hair, her dewy eyes, the tip of her nose, the dimple in her cheek, the hollow of her throat. And then his mouth found hers. He kissed her, gently at first and then with pent-up longing.

Her peacock feather drifted to the ground as she lifted her hands to caress his face and lost her fingers in his hair.

* * *

The lovers spent a tranquil hour in the garden, wrapped in the fragrance of blooming roses and serenaded by busy bees. The setting sun beamed down on them and the cloudless sky overhead stretched out across forever, its red and purple and gold pronouncing an iridescent blessing on the happy pair. But Erik and Rosamund didn't notice. They were lost in the wonder of loving and being loved.

Demurely, Rosamund voiced the age-old

question asked by every lover, "When did you know you loved me?"

Erik's eyes darkened as he recalled the poignant moment when he first realized little Rosamund had become a beautiful woman. "You smiled at me in the firelight of that poor cottage, and I suddenly knew why no girl had ever interested me. You were in my heart—had been for years." With a kiss he silenced her attempt to speak, as if to prove the truth of his confession.

When he repeated her query, Rosamund lifted her shining face to his. "I've loved you since I was a ten-year-old girl. It hurt unbearably to think you and Papa had decided my future with a business arrangement when—when I wanted to be loved. That's why I was crying in the stable."

"And threw the bucketful of feed at me?" he added, hugging her close, chuckling against her hair.

She drew back. "Oh, Erik, I *am* so sorry for the way I treated you."

His arms tightened. "Well, I'm not; now that I'm sure you love me." His reassurance erased her embarrassment, and they laughed together the way lovers do over secrets shared.

Erik plucked a yellow rose from a nearby bush and raised it to smell its sweet perfume. "A rose for my Rose," he whispered, slipping the golden bud's stem into the shining dark hair above Rosamund's ear.

She relaxed in the circle of his arms. Her smiling cheek rested against his chest, and his steady heartbeat filled her with happiness.

In her contentment she murmured, "Did you know that after you visited us at Feste Burg, I climbed the tower stairs every morning to look for your ship—yes, I did!" she insisted when he held her away in surprise. "For five summers, I did. I promised myself you'd come back for me one day."

"You darling," he exclaimed, again hugging her close. Then he burst out, "Just think, if Lord Frederick hadn't threatened your father, I'd never have come back. God certainly moved heaven and earth to bring us together." He bent to question in her ear, "And now that I'm here, how soon will you marry me?"

She raised suddenly shadowed eyes to his. "Papa has arranged for Father Andrew to come on Sunday afternoon to officiate at the funeral for my mama and the baby. If it wouldn't be too painful for Papa, we could be married the same day." Her eyes cleared with a burst of hope, "Let's go ask him?"

Erik caught his breath and reached for her hand.

***

Lord Schmidden was on his way out of the chapel when Erik and Rosamund entered, hands clasped and faces shining. He hurried toward them, but his happy words reached them first. "I see you both finally got your heads going in the same direction." He chuckled and hugged them both, one in each arm. "So, when is the wedding?" he inquired, relaxing his embrace.

"That's what we were coming to talk to you about, Papa." Worry lines creased Rosamund's forehead. "Would it be all right if Father Andrew performed the ceremony following the funeral?"

Lord Schmidden lifted his gaze to the stained-glass Shepherd in the chapel window and whispered brokenly, "It would be the very happy ending to many long years of pain." Kissing Rosamund's forehead, he turned abruptly on his heel and walked out.

Erik and Rosamund let him go, compassion drawing them into a silent embrace.

June 18, 1423. Chapel of the Shepherd, Burg Mosel.

## CHAPTER FIFTEEN

". . . in the name of the Father and of the Son and of the Holy Spirit. Amen." Father Andrew pronounced the final words of the private funeral rites for Lady Rose Schmidden."

Lord Schmidden, Lady Rosamund, and Erik Branden raised their bowed heads, brushed away their silent tears, and rose to their feet. Without speaking, they stepped into the center aisle in the chapel and moved toward the burial compartment in the left transept.

When Lord Schmidden paused by the lectern, Rosamund and Erik stopped beside him and listened while he read aloud the recent entry recorded in his own hand.

*May 21, 1412 Rose Marie Glinden*
*Schmidden and unborn infant*

*Death, suffocation.*
*Interment, June 18, 1423.*

When Lord Schmidden took a deep breath and cleared his throat, Rosamund patted his shoulder sympathetically. Then he read the final entry as his eyes followed his broad pointing finger:

*June 5, 1423 Rosamund Jeanne Abigail*
*Schmidden and Erik Branden.*
*Holy Matrimony*

Turning from the book, Lord Schmidden smiled at the young couple. "Well, what are we waiting for?"

Erik caught Rosamund's slender hand and squeezed it. His white shirt was fresh and crisp and the embroidered blue tabard that topped his well-fitting hose matched the blue of his eyes.

Wearing the purple silk *cotte* that had been her mother's and smelling of fresh honeysuckle, Rosamund embodied bridal loveliness. Her mother's pearl earrings adorned her ears, their soft touch providing the caressing sense of Lady Rose's presence.

The smiling couple moved to take their places while Lord Schmidden stepped into the corridor and instructed Curtis, "Ring the bell so everyone can join us."

* * *

While the servants assembled, Erik's eyes drifted to the Shepherd in the window and his thoughts raced back over yesterday evening's events.

Following a quiet dinner, Erik and Rosamund had joined Lord Schmidden in the great room.

"Would you play for us?" Lord Schmidden had asked Rosamund.

She immediately parted the draperies and Erik lit the candles in the candle stand that stood a short distance behind the harpsichord bench. When Rosamund slipped into her familiar place, Erik leaned against the marble wall and lost himself in admiring the lovely young woman who would tomorrow become his wife. Her charm and grace so captivated his thoughts that he took little note when Matilda entered the great room and spoke quietly to Lord Schmidden.

As Matilda disappeared through the doorway, Lord Schmidden rose and moved toward the music room. His approach made Erik straighten up, a question in his eyes. Rosamund glanced at Erik when he shifted his position, and her eyes followed his. She ended the music as her father entered the room.

Excitement roughened Lord Schmidden's voice. "A representative is here from King Sigismund. He received the message I sent recounting Erik's victory over Lord Frederick." He looked directly at Erik, "I hope he honors you well, my boy."

Erik's heart leaped, not just at the prospective honor awaiting him but at the hearty affection in the older man's tone and the adoration and pride on Rosamund's face as she stood beside him and clasped his arm in a quick, encouraging squeeze.

As the three of them moved into the great room, footsteps echoed in the corridor, tapping with military sharpness.

Matilda preceded a uniformed silver-haired gentleman and his adolescent page into the room and then halted at a respectful distance before presenting in her most formal manner, "Sir Roland, emissary from Sigismund, King of Germany, Czechia, Pomerania, Hungary, Dalmatia, and Croatia."

Sir Roland bowed politely and Lord Schmidden returned the greeting. "Welcome, Sir, and a good day to you." He gestured to the young pair standing close to him, "My daughter, Lady Rosamund, and soon-to-be son-in-law, Erik Branden."

Sir Roland nodded his acknowledgment. Then obviously a man given to efficiency, he stated his errand in clipped tones. "King Sigismund has dispatched me to bestow upon the most honorable Erik Branden the honor of an invitation to serve as a knight in the Order of Christ, upon his consent to uphold the Order's vows. Although it is protocol to invite you to spend a night in prayer before making such a binding commitment, I must leave immediately on State business, so if you will agree to the charge, I will confer the honor and be on my way."

"And what might the vows entail, Sir?" Erik inquired.

Sir Roland stated the charge. "I vow to protect the Church. I vow to fight against treachery. I vow to reverence the priesthood. I vow to fend off injustice from the poor. I vow to make peace in my province. I vow to lay down my life to fulfill these commitments."

When Erik soberly agreed to the charge, Sir Roland instructed him to kneel. Drawing his sword from its sheath, the king's representative ceremonially tapped Erik on the shoulders, first on the right and then on the left, while he recited the ritual.

"I, Sir Roland, by the authority invested in me by King Sigismund, do hereby dub you Sir Erik Branden, Knight Commander of the Order of Christ. Rise and serve in the name of God and your king."

Erik stood, tall and strong. And the suspiciously bright eyes of Matilda, Rosamund, and Lord Schmidden all reflected their pride and gratitude.

Sir Roland turned to his page and held out his hand. The young man handed a rolled parchment to Sir Roland, who broke the seal and unrolled the document with a flourish. It was inscribed with a detailed coat of arms. The heraldic charge presented a regardant deer; the crest, mantle, and motto in red; the helm in sable; and crowned and gorged in silver with a gold escutcheon from which hung an amulet engraved with a crown and Erik Branden's initials. Sir Roland read aloud the motto identifying Erik's heroism: "He who captured a fortress and burned it."

Erik felt a tremor shake his body as he reflected on the honor accorded him, and in the next moment, the pressure of Rosamund's hand on his arm brought him back from his reverie to the lovely girl beside him at the altar and the priest who would seal before God the fulfillment of his dreams and the answer to his prayers. A wife. A home. A place to belong.

* * *

*What a brave man, my papa.* Rosamund thought, observing her father's proud carriage and noble bearing while he spoke quietly with the priest. His smile came readily, and once she even heard his low chuckle. *Oh, thank you, God, for Your healing power.*

Hilde and Kathe, their faces beaming with pride, entered the chapel. Rosamund smiled at them, relieved to be reconciled to these dear folk. She'd apologized for her outburst of temper and each of the scullery maids had sought her out to make right their participation in Letty's gossip. Letty had humbly apologized for her tale-bearing tongue, and Rosamund had pardoned her, hoping the lesson would prove well taken.

She looked up at the handsome man standing motionless beside her with his eyes fixed on the Shepherd. He appeared lost in thought. When she laid her hand on his sleeve, discreetly calling his attention to the present moment, he turned his head. Their eyes met with a tenderness and affection that touched the hearts of all their friends.

As the bridal couple turned to face the altar, a hush fell over the guests. Father Andrew faithfully invited their consent, "Sir Erik Branden and Lady Rosamund Schmidden, do you come here freely and without reservation to give yourselves to each other in marriage?"

They each in turn replied, "I do."

"Will you honor each other as man and wife for the rest of your lives? Will you accept children lovingly from God, and bring them up according to the law of Christ and His Church?"

Hearing their affirmative replies, Father Andrew concluded with the charge: "What God has joined together, let not man put asunder."

Erik repeated the vow of the ring, "Rosamund, take this ring as a sign of my love and fidelity. In the name of the Father and of the Son and of the Holy Spirit." As he slipped a ring on his bride's finger, he whispered, "It was your mama's. Your papa gave it to me for you."

Father Andrew announced, "You may kiss your bride."

Erik bent his head and Rosamund lifted her face. At that moment a ray of sunlight burst through the stained glass Shepherd. It spotlighted the bridal pair, illuminating them in a fiery halo of jeweled color. It was as if God was placing His seal of approval on their union. An audible gasp echoed through the sanctuary as those present were awestruck at the tangible sign of heaven's pleasure.

It was a holy benediction, complete with God's "Amen."

The End

What *really* happened to Lady Rose? Read Book Two, *Lady Katherine*, to uncover the mystery.